FALSE FINISH

X♡X♡

FALSE FINISH

J.L. MINYARD

CENTURION
BOOKS

This book is a work of fiction. Names, characters, places, and incidents are either products of the author's imagination or are used fictitiously. Any semblance to actual persons, living or dead, events, or locales is entirely coincidental.

FALSE FINISH © 2025 by Jessica Minyard

hello@jessicaminyard.com

Cover by Cormar Covers

Interior graphics by mgsdesiigns / eBook map design by Books and Moods

Editing by Erica Edits

http://www.ericaedits.com/

ISBN: 978-1-957004-13-6

eBook ISBN: 978-1-957004-12-9

20250324

CONTENT NOTES

This book contains material that may be sensitive to some readers.

CWs: explicit sex and language, discussions of past addiction, alcoholism, sports injuries, divorce, unprotected sex, light elements of kink, gentle hand necklaces.

Dedicated to the Jessica of April 2018…who bought WrestleMania tickets for her boyfriend.

CHAPTER ONE
HARPER

Harper Myles's self-styled sabbatical was not going to plan.

She had spent the last three years busting her ass as the social media manager for a tech startup...only for the tech startup to go belly-up unexpectedly, despite her boss's many, many emails and memos and Teams messages assuring them otherwise.

She'd been unceremoniously let go—along with everyone else—with a pittance of unemployment severance.

Harper would have been more concerned—she had rent to pay on her tiny studio apartment, after all—but she had also built a pretty substantial brand as a plus-size lifestyle influencer. With her severance and the income from her channels and brand deals, she'd last a few months while she decided what and where she wanted to go next.

Harper had been nomadic after college, going wherever her heart led, documenting the journey for social media, never worried about getting attached or putting down roots, crashing at her mom's house in Nashville if she needed a quick place to stay between gigs.

Now, at twenty-five, she did not expect to find herself back in her hometown of Cedar Creek. A place she had been so desperate to leave the minute she turned eighteen.

A week ago, it seemed like a good idea. Her dad still lived here and she only saw him once or twice a year, if that. She thought they could use the time to reconnect or something like that.

She had found a cute little Airbnb to rent in historic downtown—with a secluded, fenced backyard *and* a hot tub.

She was supposed to be filming travel vlogs and shopping hauls and fall fit inspos.

She was *not* supposed to be showing up to her dad's gym because the electricity stopped working in half of her cute, ass-old Airbnb and she didn't know what to do next.

She also wouldn't have to show up if her dad answered even one of her "save me" texts.

Bluegrass Performance Center was the home of Kentucky's Independent Wrestling Association, a development territory for the bigger professional wrestling promotions, and the culmination of all her father's hopes and dreams.

BPC probably meant more to him than Harper did, although she had never put that *strictly* to the test. She had never made the man choose before.

The BPC was an impressive building that turned out to be only twenty minutes from Harper's rental.

Twenty minutes was enough time for the area to go from cute and cozy, could-be-a-set-for-a-Hallmark-movie, to nothing but rolling fields of wheat and fenced horse pastures.

The center was large, the façade made of white cement and glass windows with black framing. It reigned over the surrounding countryside and had its own spacious parking lot and manicured outdoor spaces (and a tennis court).

Harper was impressed, to say the least. And not just with the parking lot (which felt super luxurious after years of fighting for street parking). The building was sleek and modern, and her brain started to churn with content ideas. Maybe she could work with this.

The cold air blew Harper's straight bangs off her face as the doors swung open, and she was deposited into a well-appointed lobby area that was also made out of glass and sleek lines.

The woman behind the desk glanced up and gave Harper a warm smile. She had a shiny brunette ponytail and was wearing a matching sports bra and leggings—the benefits of working in a gym, probably.

"Hi! Can I help you?"

Harper glanced briefly around the woman; another set of glass doors led into the gym proper. Harper could see people and the equipment, but no sign of her dad yet.

"Are you interested in becoming a member?" The woman was still smiling pleasantly and had put a glossy brochure on the counter, presumably for Harper's perusal.

Harper raised her sharp eyebrows. One didn't usually look at her and assume she wanted to join a gym. An ex-girlfriend had called her plump. Harper enjoyed many indulgences, like pasta and ice cream and fruity cocktails, without shame or censure and she greatly disliked being sweaty. Being sweaty ruined her makeup. But the woman behind the counter didn't have the typical gym body either; she was smaller than Harper, but her thick thighs and hips filled out the leggings.

Harper took the brochure just to be polite and returned the woman's warm smile. "I'm Harper Myles. I'm here to see—"

She was cut off by the woman's squeal. "Oh, *you're* Harper!"

Harper's eyes widened. "Uh, yeah, I am."

"Teddy's girl!"

Now, she was officially in some kind of twilight zone. Her dad, Teddy Myles, apparently talked to people about her.

The woman grabbed her hand like they were old friends. "He's on the floor. Come on. I'm Raleigh, by the way, but people usually just call me Rae."

"Thanks, Rae."

Raleigh tugged her through the other set of doors, and the cacophony of gym sounds exploded around them. Harper was impressed, again, by the apparent soundproofing of the glass.

Rae led them past all the usual workout equipment—cardio machines, strength training, free weights, racks, etc., until the space opened up, revealing a twenty-foot wrestling ring.

There were two men in the ring, and two standing outside of it, seemingly in a heated conversation.

She felt Rae squeeze her hand. "I've got to get back to the desk. See ya later."

Harper could only nod, because she'd been struck speechless.

She recognized both men outside the ring.

One was her dad, Theodore "Teddy Bear" Myles, and he was gesticulating wildly at the two men grappling inside the ring.

The other man had at least four inches on her dad and was staring down at him with a severe frown on his face. His arms were crossed, and his muscles bulged out of the branded T-shirt he was wearing.

Harper would recognize that man anywhere. She had grown up watching him wrestle. He was her favorite face, and his brief heel turn in 2013 had *devastated* her. She remembered being fourteen and vowing to hate the man forever because of it.

Jesse Lee Abel, Olympic gold medalist and former heavyweight champion, was currently staring daggers at her father.

CHAPTER TWO

JESSE

Teddy Myles was an ornery old fool.

Jesse was about to tell him that—along with some other choice words—when they were interrupted by a sweet, high-pitched, "Dad?"

Both men turned towards the voice. Jesse recognized her immediately; Teddy's office desk was littered with pictures of his kid, although...the pre-teen, pre-pubescent photos were nothing like the young woman standing in front of them.

Harper Myles had grown up.

She was still short, but the tight corduroy dress she wore hugged her belly and thighs, her generous ass basically falling out from the bottom. Bright tattoos covered almost every inch of exposed skin, and her vibrant orange hair was pulled up in a messy knot. She was...loud...to look at, like some kind of exotic bird.

And it was only his second month on the job. The last thing Jesse needed to be thinking about—or noticing—was his boss's daughter's fat thighs.

Teddy, at least, seemed excited about her sudden appearance. He grabbed her immediately into a rough hug, which seemed to concern Harper.

Her heavily made-up eyes widened in surprise, and she gave him a pat on the shoulder.

Teddy released her. "Whatcha doin' here, pumpkin?"

Jesse watched Harper's lashes flutter, as if she was holding back a barely contained eye roll. It made his lips twitch, but he maintained his frown.

"I texted you three times. Why didn't you answer your phone?"

Teddy scoffed. "You know I don't like texting."

"Well, how is anyone supposed to get a hold of you?"

"You could have called."

This time, Harper's eyes did roll, as if using the phone for its original purpose—phone calls—was the biggest hindrance of her life.

She whipped the device out of her pocket. "The electric's not working in my house. I need an electrician. I was hoping you'd know a guy."

Teddy's entire weathered face lit up, as if Harper coming to him for help was the highlight of his day. He roped an arm around her shoulder. "C'mon. I'm sure I have a name or two in my office." Teddy looked at Jesse. "You good, Abel?"

Jesse inclined his head. "I'm good."

Teddy led his daughter away, and Jesse had to avert his gaze so that he didn't stare at her ass as she sauntered off.

Jesse turned back to the guys he was surveying in the ring. They were both hardcore wrestlers from a different promotion and Jesse was trying to turn them into something more refined.

Teddy liked the drama of hardcore; he thought they drew crowds. Jesse was a technician, thanks to his collegiate background.

Jesse flexed his arms and scrubbed a hand across the back of his neck, where pain still prickled. He'd been standing in one position for too long.

He wasn't paying a lick of attention to the men grappling in front of him anymore. He could blame it on the pain in his neck, that still sometimes felt like someone plunged a knife between his shoulder blades, even after all these years.

But it was something else.

It was the girl.

She hadn't even looked at him, once. And that shouldn't bother him, he shouldn't even spend one more brain cell thinking about it, but he did.

Jesse always considered himself an easy-going, level-headed man...but Harper's casual dismissal sent something cracking through his chest.

He wanted to fight.

Jesse grabbed the top rope and hauled himself into the ring. The boys—because that's what they were, early-twenties boys—stopped what they were doing and one of them grinned at him.

"What's up, old man?"

The words were teasing, but they still rankled. Jesse arched a brow. "Old man? I can still take either one of you in a match."

The boy who spoke, Ben, just grinned wider, flexing his shoulders. He was lean and ropey; Jesse probably had about thirty pounds on him.

"Wanna put money on that?"

Jesse snorted. He didn't wrestle for money anymore, but his nerve endings were on fire and he needed to do something to expel the sudden restless energy infusing his body.

He clapped Ben on the shoulder and then settled into a defensive posture. "Let's see how much you've learned."

Ben was decent, and a quick study, but Jesse still had him pinned in five moves. Jesse had them all learning Greco-Roman and freestyle because he believed that the show performances looked better if you actually knew what the fuck you were doing.

They had drawn some spectators—including Teddy—but not Harper.

Teddy was grinning at him as Jesse clapped Ben on the shoulder and then slid out of the ring.

"I thought you were just coaching," he said.

Jesse rolled his shoulders. He'd be paying for that little display tomorrow. "Yeah, well, someone has to show them how it's done."

Teddy laughed, a great, big, boisterous sound. "I knew you wouldn't be able to resist the siren call of the ring."

If only Teddy knew the full truth. If only he knew how truly painful it was to be so close to something that had been his whole life, once, and be relegated to the sidelines.

Jesse cleared his throat. Dwelling on his past regrets and mistakes and missteps never led to a good outcome. "So, what was that about? With Harper?"

Teddy shrugged. "She needs an electrician. I told her I'd call a few guys."

"Did she move back to town?"

"Just temporarily. She's got a rental on Main Cross."

Jesse's skin tingled, but he couldn't seem to stop the words he said next. "Maybe I could stop by and take a look? You know, before she pays someone."

Jesse Lee, you dumbass. That's his baby girl.

If Teddy suspected anything was amiss, he didn't show it. In fact, he sighed, like a great weight had been lifted suddenly off his shoulders. "Would you, man? I'd go, but Rae's got me booked in meetings all afternoon."

Chapter Three

Harper

When Harper answered the door, she expected a stranger—the electrician her father promised he'd call.

What she was not expecting was Jesse Lee Abel standing on her front porch.

She thought he was hot in his gym clothes. They had nothing on Jesse Lee in a tight pair of jeans and a V-cut Henley. The denim strained so hard over his thick thighs that it was in real danger of splitting.

His dark brown curls were slightly damp, like he'd just gotten out of the shower. He still wore that same severe expression, but maybe that's just what his face looked like. What was the male equivalent of Resting Bitch Face? Perpetually Scowly Face?

Jesse stared down at her intensely, his gaze seeming to mark her skimpy tank top. Harper flushed. She'd changed into something comfier for the evening—a pair of wide-legged lounge pants and a matching cropped tank, which left very little to the imagination. Especially since she'd foregone a bra.

Harper didn't care if people stared—they usually did for one reason or the other. But Jesse appeared personally insulted by her top. He clenched his jaw, a muscle flexing in his stubbled cheek.

"Jesse?" was all she managed to squeak out.

"So you do know my name," he said, his deep voice nothing more than a raspy grumble that sent heat coiling through her belly.

Harper practically bounced on the balls of her feet, her confusion at seeing him at the door gone. "Are you kidding? My dad and I practically followed you around the state when you were wrestling for IWA. I got tickets for your hardcore deathmatch for my sweet sixteenth."

Harper laughed; she was rambling now. Jesse didn't come here to listen to her fangirl about his career. So, why was he here anyway? And who told him where she lived? She should probably be more worried about those things than meeting her childhood hero.

"Um, so, why are you here, again?"

The line between his brows deepened, if that was even possible. "Your dad sent me." At her confused expression, he added, "About the electricity."

"Oh! Well, I guess you better come in, then." Harper moved out of the way so that Jesse could step into the foyer. He did so carefully, and without touching her, despite the breadth of his shoulders. She caught a whiff of his scent as he passed; he smelled clean and woodsy, like the outdoors.

He was imposing in her small space. He was too big for her two-bedroom, storybook cottage bungalow.

"What's the problem?" he grumbled.

Harper started. She had just been staring up at him like some starstruck fan. Was *starstruck* even the right term when you had the hots for your idol? Horny struck?

Harper bounced to the kitchen and flicked the switch. Nothing happened. "See? The kitchen and the dining room lights won't turn on at all. None of the outlets work either. I couldn't even make coffee this morning."

Jesse surveyed the area with his dark eyes. "Where's your breaker box?"

"My what?"

Harper swore the side of his mouth turned up, infinitesimally. It wasn't a smile or a grin or anything remotely like that, but it was something other than a frown.

"Do you have a garage or a utility room?"

Harper led him through the kitchen and to a small utility closet she hadn't even opened yet. So, she hoped it was a utility closet.

The room was tiny and cramped and packed with shelves. Jesse barely leaned into the space and opened a metal box on the wall. There were a couple black switches going the opposite direction of all the other black switches.

"Look, you just blew a couple breakers." Jesse flicked the switches a couple times and then pushed them back into the proper place.

Every light in the kitchen flared to life because she'd tried them all before texting her dad for help.

Harper leaned into the room to get a closer look at the breaker box. The movement pushed her chest into Jesse's side. He froze like a deer in headlights, all movement ceasing in his body. Harper wasn't even sure the man was breathing anymore.

"Well, would you look at that," she said, sliding her tits across Jesse's warm torso as she made a big show of examining the breaker box like she'd never seen one before. Which was technically true because that's what roommates and landlords were for.

She swore Jesse grunted before moving away from her, leaving the utility door gaping in his wake.

Harper quickly shut it, noticing that Jesse was moving rather quickly towards the front door. His long strides ate up the steps in her small house.

He was going to leave unless she thought of a good reason to keep him here. Harper's heart pounded in tandem with Jesse's booted footsteps across the hardwood floors.

"Oh!" Harper chased him through the living room. "Can I get your autograph?" She started ticking names off on her fingers. "I have Kane, Undertaker, Stone Cold, and John Cena. I'd die to add you to my collection."

Jesse looked at her like she'd lost her damn mind. And she probably had. Harper had lost all of her cool. She was usually much smoother than this. Getting dates and numbers and anything else she wanted wasn't a problem, but Jesse was something else entirely.

He gave her the slightest nod, hand falling off the door handle.

Harper practically squealed with joy. "Wait here." She needed to find a piece of paper and a pen. Harper rummaged through the different drawers in the kitchen until she found the designated junk drawer, an old notepad, and a pen with the cap chewed on. She rubbed the pen furiously on the first clean piece of paper in the notepad, just to be sure it worked, before bringing it back out to Jesse.

He was still standing in front of her door, looking displeased, hands in the pockets of his jeans, tendons straining in his forearms like he had his fists clenched.

"Here." Harper held out the notepad and pen to him.

Jesse took them both, his fingers brushing against hers. Harper tried not to visibly shiver at the warm touch.

Jesse stared at the notepad for several heartbeats and Harper had a momentary flash of panic where she thought he'd just refuse to sign after all. He was glaring at the piece of paper like the wrinkles offended him.

Then he sighed. The sound was barely audible, but Harper was watching him so closely, she caught the slight opening of his lips, the bob of his throat. He scribbled a barely legible signature on the pad, the J, L, and A swooping in big loops.

He handed the pad and pen back to Harper with the same angry scowl on his face. His eyes darted around the small house, landing literally anywhere and everywhere except on her. Which was odd. Was she really so horrible to be around? If he was so uncomfortable, then why did he come?

"Okay, well, thanks for coming." Harper's voice pitched higher than she wanted it; she sounded like a maître d' thanking someone for dining with them.

She reached past him to open the door, but Jesse must have had the same idea because his large hand caught her wrist. They both froze. His skin was hot, searing, his palm calloused and rough. Harper's breath caught in her chest when his fingers flexed.

"Why are you here?" he rumbled. It was the last thing Harper would have expected from him, and funny, she was thinking the same thing about him.

"What do you mean?"

"Why are you here? In this town?" His fingers tightened slightly on her wrist and Harper had to focus on keeping her breaths even.

"Am I not *allowed* to be here in this town?" Her gaze had been examining his large hand—the tendons roping under the sun-brown skin—but her eyes flicked to his face. He had avoided looking at her a moment ago, but now she had the full force of his attention.

The intensity of his gaze burned her insides, and she had to force herself to remain still and not rub her thighs together to ease the ache building there.

He still looked furious, but there was something else simmering there, underneath his frowny eyebrows and downturned mouth. He simultaneously looked like she personally annoyed him...and that he wanted to devour her.

It was a titillating combination that both intrigued and confused her. There was enough heat in his gaze, in the space between their bodies, that she knew he was attracted to her...but she didn't understand why he'd be so upset about that.

His eyes finally flicked away, but his hand didn't release her. "It's none of my business."

But what if I want it to be your business, she thought but didn't say. Instead, she shrugged her shoulders, like it was nothing. "I'm between jobs. I won't be staying."

He finally let go of her wrist, and Harper found that she immediately missed the searing heat of his skin.

"Good."

He practically growled the word on his way out the door, but Harper had the distinct impression his demeanor didn't have the intended effect on her, judging by the way her wet panties were sticking to her skin.

CHAPTER FOUR

JESSE

Damn Harper Myles and her skimpy tank tops.

It had been two days since Jesse had gone to her house to rescue her from a couple blown breakers. Two days of torture for him because the sight of her full tits, nipples beading under the fabric, was seared into his brain forever.

If that wasn't bad enough, she'd brushed up against him, her soft body molding so perfectly to his. Jesse wasn't able to tell whether it had been an accident or on purpose. And if it was on purpose...then why?

Jesse was almost two decades her senior, literally old enough to be her father. Why would she be brushing her tits against him on *purpose*?

It was maddening and Jesse was obsessed. It had been a long time since someone caught his attention so fully, and the hot blood coursing through his veins at the mere thought of her was almost terrifying. Devastating.

Jesse adjusted himself on the barstool, his cock hard and straining against the front of his jeans. He'd been hard nonstop for practically two whole days and refused to allow himself the relief of masturbating to the image of Harper.

She was Teddy's baby girl, and Teddy was his boss. She was off-limits.

And he was afraid of what would happen if he gave in to his urges, his fantasies. What would happen if he stroked himself to the image of her plump lips, her creamy tits? What if he imagined spurting all over her face, her chest, coating her in his cum? Marking her as his?

Well, then, he wouldn't be able to stop. He'd have to have the real thing.

A cleared throat dragged Jesse out of his reverie, and not a moment too soon. The pressure in his balls was growing uncomfortable.

"Refill, Coach?" The bartender, August, was right in front of him and Jesse hadn't even noticed him approaching. August worked at the bar and trained at the BPC; he was pretty popular on the indie circuit, but that wasn't a surprise because he was young and good-looking.

All the younger guys at the gym had taken to calling Jesse "Coach" and he couldn't decide how he felt about that. At least it was better than all the other names they could call him.

Jesse nodded and August refilled his Diet Coke from the bar.

August leaned over the bar, like he was going to start up a conversation—and Jesse didn't know how he felt about that either—but before he could start, his eyes immediately snapped towards the front door, his mouth going a bit slack.

Jesse turned in his stool to see what had gotten August so worked up, only to find his heart stuttering to a sudden stop in his chest.

Of all the goddamn places he thought he'd run into Harper Myles again, a seedy bar on the outskirts of town was not on the list. The bar—aptly named End O' Road Bar—because it was quite literally at the end of a road, wasn't an establishment you just stumbled upon.

The mystery was solved quickly because Harper wasn't alone at the door. Raleigh French, the BPC's executive assistant, was standing next to her, a couple inches taller in her wedge heels.

Jealousy gripped Jesse for a quick second before he realized Harper wasn't the reason for August's pink cheeks. Good luck to him, then. Raleigh didn't suffer fools and had been beating wrestlers and gym bros away with a stick ever since Jesse joined.

Both women were dressed like they were going to a high-end nightclub and not a dive bar in the middle of the country. Harper had on a pair of skintight jeans and one of those corset-type tops. Even from a distance, Jesse could see the sweet swell of her breasts, almost touching the bottom of her chin. Her orange hair curled softly on her shoulders.

Jesse turned back around to face the safety of the back wall. August grinned at him sheepishly before wandering off.

If he thought he would be safe facing the wall of liquor bottles, he was sorely mistaken.

The bar was not a big space.

He could hear her raucous laughter from across the room. Jesse tried not to look, but it was basically an impossible task.

He had never seen a woman unabashedly take up as much space as she did. She was a presence, a force of nature. She was loud and bright and fearless, from her orange hair to her absurdly long, glittering nails.

Jesse was not going to imagine what those nails would feel like scoring down his back. He was *not*.

Jesse was so consumed with not looking or thinking about Harper—he was staring determinedly at the bar, counting wood grains—that he didn't notice that the object of his obsession had sidled up right next to him.

Her forearm brushed his as she wedged herself between his chair and the next.

"Buy a girl a drink?"

Jesse's gaze fell immediately to her pouty mouth, which was stained a deep red. "What are you doing here?"

It was not what he wanted to say, but Jesse guessed it was better than anything else currently running through his brain.

Instead of being turned off by his attitude, the corner of Harper's mouth quirked, creating a fucking dimple.

"Rae said this is the best kept secret in town."

"Apparently, it's not that much of a secret." Jesse's tone was still argumentative, but all Harper did was laugh in that rambunctious way she had, head tipped back and tits jiggling.

When she finished, she put her hand on Jesse's exposed arm, like it was the most casual thing in the world. The touch sent sparks shooting through his skin. Her palm was impossibly warm.

He could do this. He could survive this interaction.

Jesse sighed, and it wasn't much more than a rumble. "What are you drinking?"

She pursed her lips in thought, her ridiculous nails tickling the hair on his arm. "I'll have whatever you're having."

Jesse laughed. "It's Diet Coke."

She frowned. "Are you serious? We're in a bar."

"Yeah, they serve Coke in bars too."

Her face pinched adorably, like she wasn't quite sure what to do with his response. "Fine." She waved down the bar to August, who beelined to her with a speed Jesse hadn't seen from him before. She smiled at him. "Diet Coke, please."

August didn't ask any questions, just nodded and smiled and got the lady a Diet Coke, wiping the overflow off her glass, which was a service he'd never provided Jesse.

Harper tipped the glass to her lips, and Jesse averted his gaze so he didn't stare at the way her throat bobbed.

"Ah," she said, "burns so good."

Instead of leaving, she cocked her hip and made herself more comfortable leaning against the bar. Which definitely didn't put any more space between them. Her thighs knocked against his knees, and Jesse had to adjust his position as she wormed her way in.

That was one of his worst ideas, because now she was standing between his spread legs. He slouched back, pushing at his hair in a nervous gesture.

Harper stepped closer, settling one of her arms on his shoulder, nails whispering across the back of his neck, while she swirled the glass with her other hand, ice tinkling.

"So," she started, "can I ask why you're alone in a bar drinking Diet Coke?"

Jesse could smell her now, something light and floral; the scent tickled his nose and made his balls ache. She was too fucking close. Too fucking tempting. And apparently too fucking oblivious.

"No," he growled.

He knew he was being a bore, but Harper was off-limits. It didn't matter how much he wanted her, how much he wanted to trace the rose petals that decorated her clavicles and the tops of her breasts with his fingers, his tongue. It didn't matter how much he wanted to see those red lips spread around his cock.

He wasn't going to touch her.

He'd battled two addictions and he wasn't about to get sucked into another.

Harper was frowning now, her head tilted in contemplation. "Suit yourself, Jesse Lee."

She swayed away, leaving her Diet Coke abandoned on the bar next to him.

And then, like a complete dumbass, Jesse got to spend the rest of his evening watching Harper run the pool table from across the room, tossing her hair and laughing at the dumb jokes of every guy who approached her.

He got to watch as they brushed against her body, laying hands on her hips or ass.

Jesse wasn't sure what he would do if she left with one of them. He kept clenching and unclenching his fists ineffectively...enough that August noticed and raised his eyebrows at him.

Fuck.

She was leaving with one of them.

Jesse couldn't remember the kid's name, but he'd seen him around town before. He was age appropriate for Harper. Jesse shouldn't feel anything. But instead, he felt everything, down to the marrow of his bones.

His chest was on fire as the kid wrapped his arm around Harper's soft shoulders and led her towards the door.

Jesse slung the rest of his Diet Coke back like it was hard whiskey and slammed a twenty down on the bar before stalking in their wake.

He found them on the sidewalk, too close for his liking, the boy's hand on Harper's hip, her head tipped up. She was smiling like she *liked* the guy.

"Harper," Jesse barked. Both heads swung in his direction, the guy immediately taking a step back and putting a respectable distance between them.

Jesse wasn't thinking. He was just reacting.

He stepped forward, grabbed Harper's bicep, and manhandled her around to the side of the bar, despite her protests.

She pushed him off, nostrils flaring, angry red splotches appearing in her usually porcelain cheeks. "What the fuck, man?"

Jesse stepped forward, and Harper stepped back, her back pressing against the brick. Her eyes were hard and he somehow found her anger just as compelling. He was aware that he was looming over her, but couldn't force himself to step back.

"Does your father know you're picking up men at bars?"

She jabbed him in the chest with one of her sharp nails. "I can pick up whoever the fuck I want."

"It's not safe."

"Why the hell do you care?"

She glared at him, daring him to give her an honest answer. She was a little spitfire, and her defiance made his dick hard.

Jesse stepped forward until their chests touched, her breasts pressing deliciously flush against his torso. Her face tipped up, plush mouth slightly parted. The red from her cheeks had spread down her throat.

The rhythm of her breaths changed, becoming something fluttery and frantic. Her pink tongue darted out and wet her bottom lip.

Jesse couldn't resist touching her any longer. His hand came up and he rested his palm lightly against her soft throat.

She heaved in air. He gently squeezed, just to hear her gasp.

Jesse leaned down, rasping his stubbled jaw against her soft cheek. "Go home, Harper."

And then he let her go and walked away before he could do anything worse.

CHAPTER FIVE
HARPER

Harper was used to getting what she wanted.

And what she wanted was to fuck Jesse Lee Abel.

He was rough and surly and not the best conversationalist, but his calloused hand on her throat had soaked her panties.

Harper was good at reading men, but she didn't need to work hard to decipher Jesse. The hot cock that pressed against her thigh when he had her backed against the wall spoke volumes.

The only thing Harper couldn't figure out was why he let her go. Jesse was restraining himself, holding himself at a distance. The man was locked up tighter than Fort Knox.

It was a good thing that Harper knew exactly what key would open him up.

Desperate times called for desperate measures.

Which was why she was back at the BPC with her tripod, camera, and a bottle of body oil with a line of half-naked men standing in front of her waiting for their turn.

Her dad was all about the center and as many eyes on his performers as possible. What better way to do that than a little social media campaign? She just had to whisper the words in her dad's ear and she had the temporary gig of BPC's social media manager. Her first order of business was new headshots for the guys.

"August, you're up."

She remembered August from the bar. He was a cute white guy, about mid-twenties, if she had to guess. He was wearing a tight pair of purple leggings and matching long boots.

The tight leggings were the best part.

"I can do that," he said, cheeks going pink as he eyed the bottle of oil.

"Nonsense." Harper grinned at him. Her brilliant plan wouldn't work if the guys just oiled themselves up.

August stepped close enough so that she could pour some oil on his well-defined pecs, which she then started spreading around with her hand. August's face grew redder with every pass of her hand over his nipples.

"What the fuck is this?"

Harper bit the inside of her cheek to keep from grinning. The boys jumped at Jesse's sharp tone, all of them looking extremely guilty.

She turned, just to see him storming towards them, a thunderous look on his handsome face, T-shirt straining against his biceps. She could see the bottom of his Olympic rings tattoo peeking out from the sleeve.

Harper batted her eyelashes at him innocently. "It's for social media." His frown deepened. "You know, Instagram, for the gym."

"I know what the fuck Instagram is."

He was *so* pissed and Harper was trying her damnedest not to break out in a grin. Her plan had worked almost too perfectly.

"Office. Now," he barked.

There was a chorus of snickers behind her and she could hear one of the guys say, "Oooh, someone's in trouble now" as if they were still in high school and she'd just been summoned to the principal's office.

Harper ignored them, following behind Jesse dutifully as he led the way to an area of the gym behind a door with a placard that said *Employees Only*.

Jesse was moving fast, so she didn't have time to stop and admire the well-appointed employee lounge.

He entered another room, what she assumed was the office and she followed, shutting the door behind her and flipping the deadbolt, pressing her back to the door. Her dad most certainly had a key, but Harper knew his schedule, thanks to Raleigh. They had plenty of time.

Jesse spun to face her. "They are supposed to be training. Not dicking around."

"We're not dicking around. We're working on a very targeted social media campaign. That my father approved."

At the mention of her dad, Jesse seemed to lose a little bit of his ire. He sat on the edge of the desk, crossing his ankles and thick arms. "Teddy okayed this?"

Harper walked towards him, and he eyed her warily. She stopped a hairsbreadth in front of him and leaned to the side to set the bottle of oil on the desk.

"He did." She straightened, pushing back her shoulders, which had the desired effect of bringing Jesse's gaze to her chest. She was wearing a lightweight tunic, cut in a dangerous V. "Do you have a problem with it?"

She was baiting him, daring him to object. Daring him to say he did have a problem with it, that he had a problem with her.

Jesse's rich brown eyes narrowed, his thick eyebrows drawing even closer together, if that were possible. She wanted to press on the deep line between them, massage it away, trace the crinkles at the edges of his eyes and around his mouth.

"No," he growled, his gaze on her lips.

She highly doubted that but she also really didn't care. She knew he'd have a problem with it, which made it the perfect ruse.

Harper stepped closer, bracketing his knees with her thighs. His breathing hitched; a muscle ticked in his jaw.

"Do you want to touch me?"

His expression went from angry to stricken in a heartbeat, mouth going slack but his eyes, his big brown eyes were desperate.

"Harper." Her name rumbled from his throat, maybe a plea, maybe a prayer. "I can't."

She ran one of her fingernails down the edge of the low-cut top, tugging on the fabric to expose the satin of her bra.

"You can. If you want to."

God, she hoped he wanted to. This little stunt would be awfully embarrassing if she'd read him wrong. The BPC would never see or hear from her again.

Jesse let out a strangled groan, eyes affixed on her chest. Harper's heart hammered the inside of her rib cage.

He was going to refuse. He was going to reject her.

But then his arms uncrossed, and his large hands came up and cupped her breasts, like they were the first pair of tits he'd ever touched.

Jesse molded the flesh in his palms, thumbs brushing over the skin exposed by her top. Harper's blood pounded in her head, with an echoing pulse between her thighs.

"God," he said, squeezing. He pulled down her top and scooped one of her breasts out of her bra cup.

Her nipple peaked in the cool air, but Jesse immediately covered it with his searing mouth and sucked.

Harper felt the pull of his mouth all the way through her belly. She gripped the back of his neck with her dry hand—the one not still covered in oil—long nails pricking along his skin.

He sucked and laved her taut nipple, his stubble rasping across the tender skin. She'd have a beard rash tomorrow, but it was worth it to finally have his hands on her.

Jesse released her nipple with a wet pop, and then kissed his way up her throat and across her jawline.

Harper pressed her hand to the front of his jeans and Jesse huffed out an exhale of breath. He was hard as a fucking rock. She rubbed him, feeling his erection grow under her palm. Jesse buried his ragged breathing into her neck, one hand still clutching her tit and the other on her hip.

Harper nipped at his ear; the only place she could reach. "Let me take care of you."

Jesse didn't respond; just groaned against her neck. She decisively unsnapped the button and dragged down the zipper of his jeans with one hand.

Jesse finally let go, letting her slide her hands down his body as she dropped to her knees, pulling his jeans with her.

She ran her hands over the dips in his lower abdomen, his round ass, solid thighs, letting her breath ghost over his groin. His hips bucked slightly as her fingers moved to grasp him through the fabric of his nondescript boxers.

Starting at his navel, Harper licked and sucked from belly button to the top of his boxers, following the line of soft dark hair until it disappeared. She hooked her nails into the elastic band and pulled them down, revealing the cock of champion Jesse Lee Abel.

She grasped his shaft and Jesse hissed, his head falling back and hands bracing himself on the desk.

Jesse was uncut, the glossy head of his cock already pushing through the foreskin, precum beading at the tip. He wasn't inordinately long, but he was thick, with a slight curve to the left. It was cute, endearing, as far as penises went.

Harper flicked out her tongue, licking the precum and pushing gently into his slit.

Jesse cursed above her.

She took him into her mouth, stroking the shaft and cupping his heavy balls in her other hand. She felt him grab her short ponytail; he pressed her face tighter to his body.

Harper sucked, hollowing her cheeks and relaxing her throat, so he could slide deeper inside.

"Fuck."

There was a strangled moan. The tug on her hair sent her cunt fluttering. She wondered if she could push him to be rough. She wasn't breakable. She could take whatever he could dish out.

Harper ran one of her long nails across the delicate skin of his perineum, just close enough to his asshole to tease.

"Harper, fuck, I...I can't—"

Another stroke and he was thrusting his hips, one hand in her hair and the other braced on her shoulder. His cock struck the back of her throat and she didn't flinch, just kept up the gentle pressure of her mouth, rolling his sac between her fingers.

Jesse's body shuddered and his hands tightened. Harper swallowed what she could, but cum still dripped out the side of her mouth.

Jesse jerked his hips back before she could lick him clean, stuffing his dick back into his boxers with a speed she'd never seen before. Then he was on his knees too, his big hands brushing back her hair, wiping at the tears and the cum on her face.

"Fuck, I'm sorry."

Harper laughed. "For what?"

His hands still cupped her face. His brown eyes wide and earnest, a stark contrast to his seriousness earlier. "For...this. You look..."

She knew what she looked like. She looked like she'd been sucking dick. She wanted to do more. Her body was practically begging for it, but she doubted she'd be able to tempt Jesse into fucking her on the floor. Not with that look on his face. Like he'd defiled her. Like he regretted touching her.

Of all the emotions, Harper was least prepared for that.

She cleared her throat to break the tension that had bloomed between them. "I'm fine."

She grabbed his arm to brace herself as she stood up, but Jesse was faster and still nimble on his feet. He stood and brought her with him, like it was no effort at all.

Harper brushed off her tunic and averted her gaze; Jesse's hands quickly fell away.

"Where's the bathroom?" she asked, staring at his midriff as he fixed his jeans.

"Down the hall. To your left." A pause. "Harper."

She raised her gaze and one perfect brow in question. Jesse's head was tilted, his ruddy cheeks slightly flushed. Unlike before, she could no longer read the emotion there, but his mouth was turned down again in a frown that was becoming familiar.

When he didn't finish his thought, Harper turned and left.

She'd fix her eyeliner and her attitude and be done with it.

Chapter Six

Jesse

Jesse was a right prick and if Harper never spoke to him again, he wouldn't blame her. He wasn't sure what happened, but he knew it was his fault.

He'd never had his dick sucked the way Harper did; like she was pulling his soul out of his body. It was tender and fierce and drove him wild. But then she'd looked so disheveled and he didn't want her to walk back out in the gym like that. The evidence smeared all over her face.

He'd felt shame and guilt for what he'd done. That he'd succumbed to his urges, that he couldn't tell her no.

He was old enough to be her father. He should know better. And she deserved better.

It was agony, watching her flirt with all the boys he was training, like she hadn't just been on her knees minutes before. Been on her knees for him.

There was a slight flush across her chest, but otherwise she looked exactly the same as before their tryst in the office. Teddy's office, for fuck's sake. Her lipstick wasn't even smudged.

And that was infuriating too, because Jesse couldn't even lay claim to her. She acted like nothing had happened, even though he saw the shuttering of her bright eyes and felt the distance she put between them so effortlessly.

It would haunt him for the rest of his life if he didn't put things right.

Jesse might have felt a little bit like a creep if he hadn't already been to Harper's house before.

He wasn't sure where else to find her, alone. He didn't want to confront her in the gym, because he didn't want an audience. He didn't have her number and he wasn't going to ask around, because that would surely raise suspicions. The last thing he needed was Teddy wondering why he wanted Harper's phone number.

So he waited until he was sure she'd left the BCP for the day, stopped for flowers on his way over, and showed up on her porch.

He rang the doorbell and waited.

The top of her orange head popped up in the glazed door insert and then it opened.

Harper was holding a glass of wine and wearing the skimpiest floral robe he'd ever seen. His pulse raced and his dick hardened and he had to remind himself that was not why he was here.

Her cheeks and chest were flushed, probably from the wine, and she raised her eyebrows in question, all vulnerability from earlier vanished.

"We need to talk," Jesse said.

Her eyes flicked to the bouquet he held in front of him like a shield. "Are those for me?"

"Yes," he rumbled.

Harper lifted her chin and let him in the door, heading for the small kitchen and pouring her wine down the drain, setting the dirty glass in the sink.

"I don't have any Diet Coke," she said, leaning a hip against the counter and crossing her arms, which did nothing except push her tits up and make the skimpy robe gape.

"You didn't have to do that."

"My dad's in recovery. I recognize the signs. And I'm not a bitch."

Jesse slid his hands into his pockets. So, he wasn't as slick as he thought. He knew Teddy was in recovery too, so he shouldn't be surprised that Harper caught on.

"I owe you an apology."

"For what?"

Fuck. She wasn't going to make this easy on him, was she. Jesse resisted the urge to shuffle from foot to foot like he was a scolded child under her hard gaze.

"For my behavior this afternoon."

"What about it?"

Jesse took a couple steps closer; he couldn't help himself. He was drawn to her like a moth to flames or an alcoholic who sits at a bar just to drink Diet Coke. Harper held her ground, mouth thinning, which was something he didn't like.

He liked the plush pout or the shit-eating grin or the wide spread of her lips over his cock.

"I shouldn't have let you walk out of that room without kissing you."

Then Jesse grabbed her chin and pressed his mouth to hers. He didn't have the words to say how sorry he was, or what he felt brewing in his chest, but he could show her.

There was a moment of hesitation from Harper, but then she sunk into his chest and he caught her lush body up in his free hand, even as her mouth opened underneath his. He felt her grasp at the hem of his shirt, her soft tits and stomach molding to the hard front of his body.

Her mouth was hot and she met his tongue stroke for stroke. The kiss was like a battle, with neither of them willing to surrender first.

That was fine. Jesse didn't need her surrender right now. He'd take it later, between her thighs. Harper made a devastating little sound in the back of her throat that made his dick jump.

Jesse pulled back with a groan; he was supposed to be here *talking*, convincing them both why this was such a bad idea. But with her taste in his mouth now, his reasons seemed trivial in comparison.

Harper's lips were wet, her eyes slightly glazed over. Then she smiled, those infuriating dimples popping in her cheeks.

"Get in the hot tub with me."

No, fuck, bad idea.

She tugged on the tie to her robe and pushed it off her shoulders, where it puddled at her feet. Under the robe was a tiny bikini, the pieces already slightly damp, like she'd been in the water before he showed up.

The suit was a rich blue that looked so good against her skin. It was barely three pieces of triangles, held together with little straps that hid basically nothing. Jesse could see the large, colorful tattoos on her thick thighs, the roses under her breasts and over her stomach. Her body rolled like the women in one of those old paintings in a museum.

Not that Jesse frequented museums. She was a work of art covered in art.

"I don't have a suit." It was a lame excuse and the tilt of Harper's mouth told him she thought so too.

She turned toward the back door, throwing a sultry look at him over her shoulder. "So?"

The view from the back was just as good, the little triangle cut high on her ass. She had tattoos on the backs of her thighs and one across the small of her back. She swayed out the back door and the wiggle of her ass was a siren call he couldn't resist.

Jesse put his apology flowers on the counter and stripped down to his boxers, attempting to flatten the semi that would be highly noticeable if she looked.

He prayed she would.

Even if he was terrified of what her looking would lead to next. She had already ferreted out one secret. How many more would he reveal?

Harper was already in the water by the time Jesse made it out into the backyard. Her arms were braced across the side of the hot tub, tits buoyed by the bubbling water.

It was late October in Kentucky, which meant the weather could be eighty one day and then sixty the next and you never really knew what was coming. The evening was cool, though, and Harper's nipples peaked under her top, goose bumps raised on her arms and chest.

She watched him with hooded eyes as he joined her, making himself comfortable as far away from her as possible.

She huffed a laugh. "I don't bite. Hard."

Jesse palmed his groin. It was uncomfortably tight. "We shouldn't be doing this."

She tipped her head. "We haven't done much, really."

He sighed. She was really going to make him spell everything out. "I'm old enough to be your dad."

"I like my men with a little experience."

Her voice was teasing, but Jesse didn't like her mentioning other men. He didn't want to think about anyone else touching her, not when she was so close and basically naked.

"Your dad is my boss."

She shrugged. "He doesn't have to know." She slid a little closer to him in the water, a heated look in her eyes. "What else?"

"What do you mean?"

He'd lost control of the situation because Harper had slid herself right onto his lap, warm cunt sliding over his erection. She wrapped her wet arms around his neck, those talons tickling the back of his nape. His cock twitched and he knew she could feel it. God, he wanted her so badly. Wanted to sink deep inside her, pound inside her, make her squeal. He craved her, like he used to crave the alcohol, the pills, and that terrified him the most. Terrified him more than what Teddy'd do to him when...*if*...he found out Jesse'd fucked his daughter.

Those thoughts didn't stop him from wrapping his arms around her and grabbing two handfuls of ass.

"I want to hear all your arguments against us fucking." She ground her hips down and Jesse let out a ragged moan. She ran her nose across his cheek. "That way, I can counter them and we can move on."

Jesse couldn't think. He buried his fingertips into her supple flesh. She smelled slightly like chlorine and then something floral that may have been her shampoo or perfume.

He was broken, used up. She wanted the hero, the collegiate athlete that went to the Olympics at twenty and won a gold medal. That's who she liked, who she admired, everyone did. There was a reason his ring persona was always the clean-cut, American hero.

He wasn't that man anymore.

"I'm no good for you," he rasped.

She kissed the side of his mouth. "I'm a big girl. Let me be the judge of that."

She wrapped her arms tighter around his neck, nails scraping through the short hair on the back of his head, her mouth moving fully over his.

They kissed again, and it was softer this time, more exploratory, tongues sliding together. It still made him hard. Made his hips twitch.

Harper wasn't asking for much. Maybe he could do this. He could have her once or twice and then they could go their separate ways. She was only renting; she wasn't here to stay.

Jesse dug his fingers into her hips.

"On your knees, baby girl."

Her breath stuttered out but she obeyed, moving across him on the bench seat and bracing her arms on the edge of the tub. The position raised her hips and ass to a perfect height out of the water, pale skin slightly flushed from the heat of it.

He palmed her side and didn't stop touching her as he moved his body behind hers. He skimmed down her stomach, over her hips, and then over both plush cheeks. He swatted one of them, just to watch it jiggle, and she gasped.

He notched his hands in the warm spaces between her belly and her thighs and pressed his hard cock against her ass, grinding himself in the soft flesh. Her breathing hitched and she pushed back against him.

"Would you like that? Would you like my cock in your ass?"

"God, yes," she panted.

Jesse squeezed, digging in his fingers. "That stunt you pulled at the gym was bold. How did you know I wanted you on your knees like a fucking slut?"

Where the fuck had that come from? Jesse was not normally so chatty, but there was something about Harper that brought it out. He told her he was a bad guy, so he'd show her a bad guy.

His words did nothing except make Harper whine and squirm against him.

As much as he craved to bury himself balls-deep in her, there was something he needed to do first.

He slid a hand between their bodies and fingered her cunt through her swimsuit bottoms.

"Jesse," she whined.

He liked the desperation in her voice. He liked his name in her mouth.

He smacked her ass again. "Don't move, or you won't get what you want."

She made another desperate sound, body quivering with restraint.

Jesse pushed the bottoms aside, exposing her slit to the air. In the dusky evening, he couldn't see the color of her cunt, but he could imagine the soft pink folds. His fingers would have to be enough for now.

He ran a finger through her, to find her soaking. Harper whimpered but didn't move, like she'd been told. He toyed with her, rubbing his finger through her arousal, brushing over her engorged clit. He thoroughly soaked his finger before moving to the puckered hole of her ass and pressing gently.

Harper bucked and he *tsked*. "I thought I told you not to move."

He went deeper, just up to the first knuckle, but he had thick fingers and Harper moaned beautifully but kept her hips still this time. With two other fingers, he found her clit easily, the little nub slick and puffy. He rubbed her in fast circles, pressing his body to hers so that she could feel his cock as he fingered her.

"Look at you," he said. "So wet and wanting. Do you like that, baby girl? Are you going to come with my finger up your ass?"

Harper let out a strangled breath, her arms shaking where she braced on the side. He wanted her to come around his cock but there would be time for that later. He wasn't leaving this house until the girl couldn't walk.

Jesse felt Harper's cunt throbbing under his palm and she came all over his fingers with a cry.

CHAPTER SEVEN
HARPER

Harper had unleashed something in Jesse.

He definitely gave off stern brunch daddy vibes, but she had expected him to be a more straightlaced, missionary type of guy. She was not expecting to be spanked and then fingered within an inch of her life.

And the way he called her "baby girl" did something delicious to her insides.

After he'd made her come so hard she saw stars, he helped her out of the hot tub and wrapped her in her robe, like she was something fragile and precious. What did she have to do to get him to realize she was *not* breakable?

Since his boxers were good and soaked, Harper gave Jesse a towel to wrap around his cut waist and then she made them both coffee.

He turned up his nose at her pumpkin spice creamer, though, just taking his plain.

They stared at each other from opposite ends of the kitchen as they sipped their drinks. Awkward.

Jesse had color high in his cheeks and he kept shooting her hot glances that made Harper rub her thighs together. Jesse didn't miss that movement, either.

Harper took a couple sips of her coffee before abandoning the mug on the counter. "Well, I'm going to go change into something dry before I get a yeast infection."

She grimaced, even as she headed towards the stairs. *Good job, Harper. You want him to fuck you, not run away screaming because you're talking about infections.*

The bedrooms were on the second floor of the house. They were small, but cozy.

She stripped off the damp robe and wet suit, dropping them both to the floor.

"Get on the bed."

Harper's heart slammed into her chest. She had heard Jesse following her, but he stood in the doorway, buck naked. He leaned a shoulder casually on the frame, as if his cock wasn't bobbing in the air for all to see.

She sucked in a breath and sat on the edge of the bed.

"Spread your legs." His voice was deep and raspy and sent a shudder down her spine. She felt like he had sucked all of the air out of the room.

Harper leaned back on one hand and spread her knees slowly.

Jesse's molten gaze followed the movement until her center was fully exposed for his view. Harper could feel his eyes like a weight against her center. Her body heated, nipples hardening in the air and pussy clenching in expectation.

Her breasts were heavy and achy and with one hand, Harper plucked at a nipple just to watch Jesse's jaw harden.

His biceps flexed as he ran a hand down his shaft.

Jesse had always been a good-looking guy. In his twenties, he was every teenage girl's wet dream. In his forties, his features had hardened and grown more refined with experience. He was rugged and chiseled and looked like he'd be more at home on a mountain instead of coaching in a gym. His chest was still sculpted with rolling muscle, but he had thickened out around the stomach, which Harper enjoyed immensely.

She skimmed her palm down her abdomen, over the patch of curls that covered her mound, and spread her lips for him with two fingers.

Jesse let out what could only be described as a growl, his nostrils flaring, hand moving faster.

Harper's breathing matched the cadence of his, the rapid rise and fall of his chest, as the pads of her fingers found her clit.

"Show me, baby girl. Show me what you look like when you come."

Harper's chest heaved as she rubbed hard circles around her clit. She wasn't interested in the slow tease anymore. She wanted to feel the climax rip through her hard and fast and urgent. Harper moaned and closed her eyes as the sensation built.

But then her hand was snatched away. She cried out in shock and frustration as her body throbbed with unsatisfied need.

"No," Jesse said. He was right in front of her now, hand clamped around her wrist. "Don't close your eyes. Look at me when you play with your pussy."

He released her hand and stared at her. They were almost nose to nose; Harper could feel his warm breath on her lips. A little whine escaped as her fingers found her clit again. She rubbed, eyes never leaving Jesse's.

It was hot. So immensely hot. He was all she could see, all she could smell, all she could feel. The orgasm built again quickly, Harper's breaths coming in sharp gasps.

"Look at you," Jesse drawled. "So eager to please."

Then he stuck two thick fingers inside her. Harper yelped in surprise, but it quickly became an unrestrained moan, because that was exactly what she needed. To be stuffed full of him in any way. The orgasm crested and broke, her cunt clenching and grasping around his fingers, which stroked her insides with firm precision. He pressed a little deeper, until he was stroking the spongy front of her vaginal wall, even as she still convulsed.

Harper fell back on the bed and Jesse followed, his torso pressing into hers, fingers still stroking. She grabbed his arms.

"Jesse," she panted. "Jesse, I can't, I can't." She felt almost delirious in pleasure. She squirmed and bucked against his hand, but his fingers didn't stop.

His stubbled jaw brushed against hers. "You can, baby girl. Give me one more pretty orgasm. I know you can do it."

Harper was really done for now. She knew she didn't look sexy or composed. She was wild. She could feel the sweat building on her chest and across her forehead. She couldn't draw a full breath.

Jesse twisted a fistful of hair in his iron grip to stop her thrashing, holding her body still with the weight of his as he rubbed and stroked and pressed until she was practically screaming. She orgasmed again, the sensation almost painful this time.

"Oh, fuck." She could barely breathe. She could feel the pulsing of her cunt in her chest, her wrists, the femoral arteries in her thighs.

Jesse kissed her softly, tenderly, on her cheeks, her mouth. The hand in her hair brushed damp strands away from her forehead, while the one that had stroked her so furiously rubbed the insides of her thighs.

"Where are your condoms?"

Harper laughed breathlessly. "You didn't come prepared?"

She saw Jesse's mouth curve a fraction of an inch. "I didn't want to assume."

She could feel his hard, hot cock leaking onto her thigh. She nodded towards the dresser. Jesse went to fetch the condom and she felt a moment's longing at the absence of his warmth on top of her.

Harper crawled more fully on the bed, her arms and legs feeling like jelly. Her pussy was still fluttering, even as her heart raced with anticipation.

Jesse slid the condom on with smooth efficiency, and then knelt beside her on the bed. Harper's limbs spread languidly, her thighs falling apart for him automatically. He fondled one of her breasts with a casual, proprietary tenderness.

"I didn't hurt you, did I?"

She smiled up at him. "You're going to have to try a lot harder than that."

An unknown emotion flashed in his eyes, the barest flicker of dark longing that sent her heart racing. There were apparently many layers to Jesse Lee Abel, and Harper looked forward to uncovering them all.

She stretched her arms above her head, Jesse's hungry gaze following the way her breasts moved. She'd felt how hard he was. He had to be positively aching at this point. Why was he still hesitating?

She ran a hand over his bicep, over the black ink of his Olympic rings, tracing each circle with her nail. "Jesse Lee, if you don't fuck me right now, you're going to have to leave and I'll get my vibrator to finish the job."

He let out a raspy chuckle at that, maybe the first laugh—if you could call it a real laugh—she'd heard from him so far.

He captured her mouth, settling his big body between her thighs. His cock notched easily at her entrance. "Well." He pressed in, just enough to tease. Harper bit at his bottom lip. "When you put it that way."

With a hard thrust, he sheathed himself fully inside. They gasped in unison.

"Goddamn," Jesse cursed, his brow furrowing.

He looked fucking pissed again, but Harper wasn't going to take that personally because his hips were undulating, his thickness a delicious stretch. She was more than ready for him, though, her first three orgasms making her impossibly slick and her body languid.

Jesse's first few strokes were unhurried, tame. Harper dug her nails into the hard muscles of his ass, which earned her a hard thrust that stole her breath.

"Fuck, Jesse, harder."

His eyes were almost wild. Two deep, dark pools.

Jesse adjusted his body, pushing her thighs to her chest, and then he grabbed two bars of the wrought iron bed frame. He ground his pelvis against her, once, just so she could feel the whole of him inside her.

The pace he started next was brutal, fierce. Harper could do nothing but lie there, gasping for air, her soft body absorbing the impact, wet skin slapping together.

It was exhilarating, feeling the power in his body, watching him unleash a part of himself that he kept so closely tethered. Harper's cunt fluttered and clenched around him; this fucking man was going to make her come for a fourth time tonight.

He reached down and fondled one of her breasts roughly, calloused palms chafing across her sensitive nipple. Harper ran her palms up his abdomen and left them there, so that she could feel the rolling of his muscles, feel the way they tightened with his own impending release.

"So. Fucking. Pretty." He punctuated his words with hard thrusts. The hand on her breast moved down her body until he could finger her clit and that was all it took. Her orgasm exploded, shaking Harper's body.

Jesse released the headboard, his body falling down to cover hers, one hand still on her clit while the other wrapped in her hair. His mouth and tongue were on her neck. Jesse practically growled as he came, his hips pumping short and erratic inside her.

They were both out of breath, chests heaving and slick skin stuck together.

Harper tried to get off the bed and head to the bathroom to pee and shower, but Jesse's sturdy arm wrapped around her middle and dragged her back down on the bed. He tucked her into his side, heavy leg slung over hers. He wiped some sweaty hair off the side of her face and buried his nose in the crook of her neck.

Oh, so they were snuggling.

That was unexpected. Harper hadn't snuggled in a hot minute. She wasn't really the snuggling type, but had to admit it was kind of nice to just bask in the warmth of his body for a while.

Jesse's hand roamed leisurely over her arms, the side of her stomach, her upper thighs. The calluses on his palms raised goose bumps. It wasn't a touch to arouse, though, more that he just wanted to feel her.

His finger traced the outline of one of the tattoos on her arm, much like she'd done to him earlier. "Why so many?"

Harper shrugged. "I just like them. They're pretty." At this point, Harper had lost count of how many tattoos she had, especially the little ones. Some were sentimental, some were mementoes from places or people or events, some were just for fun.

She'd gotten her first tattoo with an older boyfriend when she was seventeen and they'd lied about her age. Harper had always looked older, acted more mature, according to him. So now she had a stupid character from a video game on the back of her calf and she didn't even play video games. She didn't regret many of her tattoos, but that was one she could do without, even if she did forget it was there most days.

"What's this one mean?" Jesse's fingers had stopped somewhere along her arm.

Harper had to crane her head to look at which one he was referring to. She laughed. "I just like frogs, man."

Jesse smiled, but he was still looking at the fat toad on her arm. It was almost just for himself, the curve of his lips soft and contemplative. Something about that expression made Harper's chest ache.

This was just supposed to be about sex. Two people who had the hots for each other rubbing one out. She had been flirting with Jesse since he showed up to her house to fix the electricity, and this was the culmination of all those little interactions. Wasn't it?

She was just renting this little house until her next permanent gig came along. She had no desire to move back to this small town, with its familiar places and familiar people. She had outgrown it, outgrown them.

Harper would have to keep repeating that mantra to herself, even as Jesse gazed down at her with something akin to wonder on his face.

CHAPTER EIGHT

JESSE

Harper didn't know it—at least, he was pretty sure she didn't know it—but he was dating the fuck out of her.

Jesse hadn't dated anyone in a long time, so his skills were a bit rusty, but he was almost positive that's what it was still called. They saw each other almost every day, he spent the night at Harper's house, and she brought him ridiculous flavored coffee on the mornings she came to the gym.

He wasn't exactly sure what an influencer did or what a social media campaign was, but whatever it was, it required Harper to be at the gym with her camera and tripod almost every day. Jesse wasn't going to complain about that because that meant he got to spend his days watching her and listening to her laugh, even if his balls shriveled up every time Teddy looked at her with that proud father face.

There were two things they didn't talk about: Teddy and the expiration date on whatever *this* was that they were doing.

Jesse knew she was just passing through. She didn't want to be here, in the sleepy town that raised her. Jesse's head knew that, rationally, but his traitorous heart beat a little faster at the idea of her staying. Staying because she wanted to, because *he* was here.

But there was an insidious little voice in the back of his mind that whispered the truths he always knew. He wasn't good enough for her. He was damaged goods, washed-up. She deserved so much more than a washed-up ex-professional wrestler, addict in recovery.

He was almost afraid that instead of alcohol or pills, he was drowning his sorrows in Harper, in her plush body, hot cunt, and the little sounds she made when she came.

The air suddenly *whooshed* out of his lungs as August landed a punch to his gut.

The boys hooted with good-natured heckling.

August was bouncing in front of him, face sweaty and red from exertion. "Distracted, Coach?"

Jesse took a minute to recenter himself. Whatever was going on with Harper could wait. He was in the middle of the ring. He was good at compartmentalizing. He tapped his gloves together. Took a steadying breath. Let his lungs expand and his awareness travel down his extremities. His arms and legs and fists knew what to do, he just had to let them.

"Not on your life, kid. Again."

August started bobbing and weaving in front of him, his steps too fast and erratic. He was too quick, reckless, impulsive.

Jesse weaved, biding his time, waiting for the perfect opening in August's guard. There. *Kids.*

Jesse's arm struck out and he hit August with a quick jab-cross-hook to the boy's helmet. August stumbled, and Jesse retreated so he could get his bearings again.

There was commotion from the side that drew Jesse's attention and one of the boys said, "Girls are here," in a voice that implied he had never seen girls before.

Harper and Raleigh were indeed huddled conspiratorially together not far from the ring. Harper was wearing another one of those infuriatingly short skirts that fluffed around the bottom of her ass. At least she had tights on this time, though.

Jesse pulled at the straps of his gloves with his teeth. "Ben, come take my spot. I better see one of you land a punch correctly before I get back."

He slid out of the ring and prowled towards the girls. He thought he had on a serious enough expression—they were being a distraction—but Harper just smiled up at him and batted her unnaturally long lashes. She was not cowed.

"What?" he snapped.

"Surlier today than normal, huh, Coach?" Raleigh said, the smartass.

Harper's lips just dipped in that mischievous little smirk she had. "I need your help at the house."

Jesse frowned. "What's wrong?"

"Well, how am I supposed to know?" she said flippantly.

Jesse grumbled, looking back over his shoulder at the motley bunch of amateur wrestlers he was supposed to be training. They'd be okay for a minute—probably. He could run to Harper's house and be back in thirty minutes, as long as she hadn't set something on fire.

"Fine. Give me ten."

Harper's eyes sparkled with something suspiciously like triumph. "I'll wait for you in the lobby."

Jesse showered quickly in the locker room and changed into his jeans and boots. He found Raleigh and Harper in the lobby, just like she'd said.

"Keep an eye on them, yeah?" He nodded towards the gym. Raleigh gave him a thumbs-up.

He followed Harper to the parking lot, her hips swaying in her little skirt.

"Are you going to tell me...What the fuck?"

Harper had spun around and pinned him to the side of his pickup truck, her hands on his ass and her mouth on his throat. Jesse tried—and failed—not to sag into the touch. Her soft body grinding into his was all he could think about.

"Harper, what about—"

She pushed up on her toes to snag his bottom lip with her teeth. "I lied."

His hands circled her waist—he should push her away, they were still in viewing distance of the damn front doors—but he just ended up pulling her closer. He was already half-hard, fuck. Jesse groaned.

"About what?"

She nipped him again, and desire sparked down his spine. "About the house. I just wanted to see you."

Something other than desire curled through Jesse's abdomen, but he'd just ignore that particular feeling.

"I'm working."

She palmed his erection. "Do you want me to go?" There was something bright and sharp and defiant in her gaze. It was the kind of look that made him want to bend her over and smack her ass until she was breathless before burying himself in her heat.

His fingers spread across the small of her back. "No."

She smiled. "Take me somewhere."

"Get in the truck."

When Jesse started driving, he didn't have a specific destination in mind. He just had the strongest urge to show her all the beautiful parts of the countryside. He wanted her to see the cornstalks, the sunflower fields, the soybeans, the quiet serenity of a one-lane backwoods road.

Harper had her window down, her pale arm riding the breeze, orange hair whipping around her face like tiny flames. Her eyes were closed, face relaxed and sweet.

Jesse eventually pulled the truck over on the side of the road.

Harper's head swiveled around. "We're just going to park here?"

Jesse hid a smile. "No one will bother us, city girl."

She gave him a look, her little nose wrinkled. "I grew up here." Her tone was almost indignant.

"I know," Jesse said, helping her slide out of the truck. They were parked on a bit of an angle, the bank sloping away from the road.

Harper slipped her hand into his, entwining their fingers, stepping delicately over branches and brambles in her shiny black heeled boots.

"You know, when I said take me somewhere, I meant more like a pumpkin patch or the bookstore, not, like, the woods."

Jesse snorted, but Harper was still going.

"I'm not really the woodsy type. What if I get bitten by a tick?"

"I'll check you for ticks later."

She pursed her lips, clearly not finding his levity at the tick situation amusing. Jesse just shook his head.

They didn't have to walk far. The trees broke open to reveal a slowly moving creek. Shafts of sunlight slanted through the sparse tree coverings, dappling the water. Down here, the bank was mostly river rocks, covered with slick moss and algae. Jesse found a decently flat rock and brushed the surface off with his hand.

"Yes, that helped," Harper quipped, but she sat down anyway, dipping the toes of her shiny boots in the water and then flicking them, water droplets arching through the sunlight.

Jesse sat down behind her, digging his heels in the soft loam, bracketing Harper's body with his thighs. She hugged his knees.

They were quiet, listening to the sounds of the creek, the wind rustling through the leaves.

"My dad used to bring me here, growing up. We would fish and catch crawdads when the water was low."

"I know."

"How?"

"You talked about it in an interview one time. Right before a pay-per-view cage match, remember?"

Jesse could barely remember. That was before one of his last events before he officially retired. He'd been high as a fucking kite during most of the interviews during that time.

"You know everything about me, then."

He wrapped his arms around her so she would lean further into his chest. She was warm, while the air was chilly.

"Not everything."

"What else could you possibly want to know?" He cupped both of her breasts, since his hands were right there anyway, testing their weight, enjoying the way his touch changed Harper's breathing. He knew it was dangerous territory, opening up his life like that, basically daring her to ask questions.

"Why'd you quit?"

Jesse's hands stilled. "I didn't quit. I retired."

He heard her exhaled breath as she scoffed. "They're basically the same thing. You were at the height of your career."

"I was old."

"There are performers older than you still working."

This was why he didn't date, didn't get attached. This was why he knew better than to get involved with someone like Harper, who was basically born and raised in the game. She knew how the system worked.

What was he supposed to tell her? That he stopped being able to pass the drug tests and his manager could no longer cover for him because it was becoming too obvious? That the company gave him a choice? His reputation and his career or his secret?

Jesse stood abruptly, jostling Harper a little more than he intended to on the way up. She let out an indignant huff.

"Jesse, what the fuck—"

But he was climbing, he needed to get back to his truck, clear his head, reorganize his thoughts.

He was climbing and then the heel of his boot hit a particularly slick patch of moss and then he was falling face-first into the dirt with an undignified grunt.

Harper squealed. But she came to his side anyway and helped Jesse roll over and wipe the mud and leaves and sticks off his face and the front of his shirt.

"Are you okay?" Her brows were knitted, concerned for his well-being even after he basically knocked her over first.

Jesse grunted. He swore he saw the flutter of her eyes rolling, but then she was grasping his elbow to help him to his feet. Jesse hissed as her soft hands brushed his wrist.

Harper missed nothing. She pushed up his sleeve to reveal redness starting up his forearm. Jesse tried to flex it, but pain shot up through his elbow and he had to grit his teeth to keep from making more noise.

"I'm fine," he said.

"Stop. You are obviously not fine."

She wedged her shoulder under his armpit, like not being able to use his wrist would hinder his ability to walk. And maybe she was right since he'd just tripped going uphill.

Jesse let her bear a bit of his weight just because he liked the feel of her pressed up against his side. And he'd hold on to that feeling as long as he could.

CHAPTER NINE
HARPER

Harper knew Jesse was hiding something, but she couldn't discern what it was or why he felt like he needed to keep it hidden so badly that he risked bodily harm.

If Jesse's face wasn't contorted in pain, Harper would have been laughing at the sight of him falling face-first in the dirt. She figured he'd been humiliated enough and didn't need her rubbing salt in the wound, so she held her tongue while he drove them to an urgent care one-handed.

Jesse had refused to let her drive his truck, but he capitulated to seeing a doctor. She wasn't going to let him just go back to work, despite his protests.

They pulled up in front of a small, squat building that was in the middle of the town square, directly across from the chamber of commerce.

Harper narrowed her eyes. "This isn't urgent care."

Jesse just grunted. "It's fine. Dr. Bennett has a background in sports medicine." At her continued suspicious look, he added, "She comes out to the gym sometimes."

"I guess that's better than nothing," Harper mumbled.

She helped Jesse get out of the truck and get his keys stuck in his pocket; he was holding his arm across his chest, elevated above his heart.

The doctor's office may have been small, but it was cute and homey on the inside. They didn't have to wait long before a medical assistant led them back to one of the three exam rooms and took Jesse's vitals. No one questioned Harper's presence, so she just hung out at his shoulder, twisting the front of her skirt in her hands.

"Jesse Lee!" the doctor exclaimed when she came in. Dr. Bennett was a tall woman with a slick auburn ponytail and hot pink scrubs. She sat on the stool, snapping on gloves and spinning in towards them. Harper found she liked the woman immediately. "Didn't think I'd be seeing you in here. I thought you knew better," she chided.

Harper watched the tops of Jesse's ears turn slightly pink. "Yeah, shit happens."

Dr. Bennett held out her hands for Jesse's wrist, pulling a pair of glasses out of her hair. "What, exactly, happened?"

When Jesse didn't immediately reply, Harper decided to help him with the details. "He fell on it. In the woods."

A sly smile curved the woman's lips. "A sex injury? Why, Jesse Lee, you old dog."

Jesse looked like he wanted to crawl out of his skin and disappear, but Harper just laughed. She really liked Dr. Bennett now.

"Unfortunately not."

Dr. Bennett's sharp gaze cut to her. "You're Harper Myles, right?"

Harper nodded. She'd forgotten how news got around in this town. But Dr. Bennett didn't make any further comments, about her or about them showing up together at her practice.

She finished her quick exam of Jesse's wrist. "Well, you know I can't definitively say it's not broken without an x-ray, but I think you're lucky and just sprained it. How's the pain?"

Jesse flexed his fingers even as he grimaced. "Improving. And there's no numbness."

"I can send you home with a temporary brace and some painkillers."

"No meds." His voice was a low rumble.

"Call me if it gets worse, okay?" She grinned, eyes flashing between the two of them. "And no more shenanigans in the woods. Doctor's orders."

"I'll keep an eye on him," Harper said. She went to place her hand on his shoulder, but Jesse shrugged away from the touch. It wasn't super obvious—she doubted Dr.

Bennett even noticed—but it was enough for Harper to pull her hand down.

The movement had been small enough that Harper could rationalize it away. Maybe Jesse hadn't realized she'd been reaching for him. But there was another part of her that whispered that the move had been deliberate. That he didn't want to be connected to her in public, even though she was standing right next to him in the room. The touch was too intimate, and assumed too much.

It made her heart ache in a way she wasn't expecting.

Jesse drove Harper home because her rental was only one street over. She'd have to get back to the BPC sometime to retrieve her own car, but right now, Harper needed a minute to think.

Jesse followed her into the house in more sullen silence; she heard the snick of her door as he closed it behind them.

Harper rounded on him. "Listen, if we're going to make this work—"

His hot, angry gaze speared her. "Make what work? You're leaving."

She deflated before getting the chance to really gear up for an argument. Because he wasn't technically *wrong*. She just wasn't sure he cared that much.

Yes, this was supposed to be some temporary fun and a temporary arrangement. Her house was just supposed to be temporary, her work at the BPC temporary. Even though she had stopped looking for permanent jobs weeks ago. That had been an easy decision. She was seeing results on her own platforms, with her own content. She was seeing the results from her work with the BPC. August had already been booked by one of the bigger promotion companies for some house shows. She had done that; she had made that happen. The changes she had been seeing were making her reconsider finding full-time work at someone else's company.

The numbers were making her seriously consider just being a freelancer and a full-time influencer. She could pull it off, if she worked hard enough.

She hadn't shared that with anyone yet, though.

"So, you're just gonna throw me away like you threw away your career?"

Jesse flinched at her hard words. They were mean, Harper knew that, but she was hurt and wanted him to know how much. She wanted him to *feel* how much she hurt, even though she wasn't sure he felt anything at all, at least for her.

Muscle ticking in his jaw, Jesse moved past her and slumped down on the couch. It wasn't what she expected him to do next.

He was still silent, but he wasn't leaving.

Jesse leaned his elbows on his knees, scrubbing his face with his uninjured hand.

Well, this was her house. She couldn't storm out of her own damn house. Harper nibbled on her bottom lip.

Jesse was different from the other people she'd dated, and she had dated a broad spectrum of different types. There was a delicate vulnerability that cloaked him like a shadow, despite his stoic, grumpy exterior.

Harper made up her mind.

She walked towards him. Careful of his wrapped wrist, she settled herself over his lap, one knee on either side of his broad thighs.

She cupped his face in her hands. She kissed the hard lines that creased his forehead, then she tucked his face into her neck.

Jesse made a strangled sound in the back of his throat, his hand fisting the back of her skirt.

She scraped her nails down his nape. "Just talk to me, Jesse. Baby, please."

His breath fluttered across her neck as he released a ragged sigh. Harper wasn't sure this would work, either. But she was willing to sit on him and stroke his neck until he said something, anything.

Jesse's lips ghosted over her skin and she shivered.

Harper had thought there was nothing left for her here, in this small town, but maybe, just maybe, there was Jesse.

CHAPTER TEN
JESSE

Confessing his sins while Harper sat on his dick was not the worst thing to ever happen to him. He'd endured more, suffered more. If there was ever a time to be truthful, now would be it.

Jesse knew he'd hurt her feelings when he pulled away from her touch in the exam room. He couldn't help himself. She may have forgotten how small towns worked, but he never could. It would only be a matter of time before news spread that they'd been seen together. Dr. Bennett knew Teddy; she treated his athletes on a regular basis. Fuck, half her office had dated half his gym, to several spectacular blowups.

He could probably come up with some half-assed excuse for why they were there together, but not if they looked like they were...together.

A small part of his brain wondered if that would be a bad thing. If everyone knew, they could finally stop with the subterfuge, something Jesse was not any good at.

But if everyone knew, they'd have to put a name to whatever it was that they were doing.

Jesse nuzzled deeper against the soft skin of her neck. She smelled sweet. Tasted sweet. She called him *baby*, like it meant something.

He closed his eyes, dug his fingers into the soft flesh on her hip.

"Do you remember my match at the Riot Time special?"

He felt her nod, her nails raking down the back of his neck like he was a wild horse in need of soothing. And maybe he was, because why did that little movement feel so fucking good.

"The finisher was a German suplex. Nothing fancy. I'd taken a thousand of them before, but something went wrong." Jesse's voice was raspy and tight. The memory still burned. "I messed it up or Henry Parker messed it up. I don't think we'll ever know. But I couldn't move." Jesse remembered the pain had been severe, but it was the fear that had kept him paralyzed. He knew immediately he'd hurt something, but the fear had been a living weight on his chest; he couldn't move, couldn't breathe. He remembered the whites of Henry's eyes too; Henry's fear, that must have been reflected on his own face.

"I remember," Harper said softly. "It was a shock. Everyone thought you were going to win that match."

"I was. I was supposed to kick out of the pin on the second count." A false finish is what they called that, a dramatic turn before the actual end of the match. Except everyone in the ring could tell Jesse wasn't getting up and they had to call the match against him. "I was in recovery for six months, but the pain just wouldn't end, no matter the dosage or the type of painkiller. And we tried them all."

Jesse was no stranger to pain. He'd been an athlete—football, rugby, wrestling—since he could walk. But he'd never sustained an injury of the kind he'd taken in the ring that day. Every time he went to the doctor and complained about his neck, the doctor would refill or increase his dosage, no questions asked. When they should have been asking questions about why he was going through them so quickly.

It was a slow, irrevocable descent.

Jesse inhaled Harper's scent. Her skin always smelled faintly of coconut, which reminded him of sunshine, of the beach.

"That wasn't your fault," she said.

"I tried to come out of it, but it was too late. I was stuck in the high. If I wasn't using pills, the pain was unbearable.

My manager told me it was fine, that I just needed to push through. So I did."

She brushed her fingers through his hair. "You're not defined by one mistake, Jesse."

"It wasn't just once. It happened over and over again. I could have hurt someone." If he was honest with himself, that's the part that haunted him the most. It wasn't the addiction. It was the guilt that ate away at his insides. He'd been stone-cold sober for five years, and it still felt like at any time, at any moment, he could be dragged back down again. "I couldn't pass the drug tests anymore. My manager dumped me. They gave me an ultimatum. I could retire quietly or they would fire me for breach of contract. And then everyone would know."

There. That was it. All of Jesse's secrets laid at her feet for her judgement.

Harper pulled back, grasping his face in her small palms. Her eyes were bright and red-rimmed, like she was going to spill tears for him.

"They should have gotten you help," she said, angry on his behalf.

Jesse's lips twisted wryly. "I should have gotten myself help, long before I finally did. Rock bottom is a hard place to land. And an even harder place to crawl out of."

Her thumbs brushed over the arches of his cheekbones. "I know. I know what this profession does to people, to families. You know my dad."

Jesse did. He knew Teddy battled his own demons and had for a very long time. He knew Teddy's wife—Harper's mom—left him and it took him a month to notice because he traveled so much. The blogs and the podcasts and the news had dragged him and his family through the mud.

"I did throw away my career, Harper. And you have no idea what it feels like to lose everything."

Her mouth pursed. "I'm the only child of a contentious divorce. I do know a little bit about loss."

"I suppose you're right." His good hand flexed on her hip.

She kissed his forehead tenderly, then, with a twist of her lips that was both sweet and mischievous, she slid off his lap.

Jesse missed the heat of her body instantly, but then she started pulling off her shirt and he felt marginally better.

She had on a lot of layers, so it took a minute for her to discard them all. Jesse chuckled when she tripped taking off one of her boots and she gave him the finger while her tits wiggled. He had to adjust his position on the couch as his cock swelled.

Completely naked, she grinned at him, fluffing her sunset orange hair over her shoulders. She was a fucking masterpiece, his own little goddess walking among mortals. He wanted to worship every dip and curve and dimple of her luscious body; the little rolls down her sides, the crevice of her belly, the creases of her thighs. He wanted to steal her away and keep her completely to himself, making her come over and over and over again while she screamed his name until she couldn't scream anymore.

Harper reseated herself on his lap and Jesse couldn't help the groan dragged out of his throat. His sore wrist throbbed in time with his dick. He traced a line up her spine just to feel her shiver under his hand.

She sighed into his chest, snaking her arms around his neck and kissing the side of his mouth. She teased him with her tongue, softly. He let her explore his mouth for a minute, just enjoying the way she felt in his arms, the way her breath hitched even though he wasn't doing anything to her yet.

"Unbuckle my pants," he growled. Air puffed out of her chest as her hands dove towards his belt and the button on his jeans. The way she took orders in bed made his balls ache.

He leaned back so she could reach his button and zipper. One of her nails caught on his shaft and he sucked in a breath.

"Oops," she said, cheeks tipped pink, little grin on her lips.

Fuck, she was so bratty and sensual and fucking perfect. The pads of her fingers slid up his aching cock until he couldn't take it anymore.

He pushed her off his lap and she landed on the couch with a huff, but he covered her with his body, tucking his injured wrist between her body and the back of the couch.

He was between her thighs, which was quickly becoming his favorite place on earth.

Harper arched up into him. "Jesse, please," she pleaded.

He wasn't going to make her wait, not when she looked so pretty underneath him and asked so politely, skin flushed red and glowing.

Jesse latched onto one of her dusky nipples and sucked hard while plunging one finger inside her hot, warm cunt. She whined at the intrusion, gripping his head and shoulder with her nails. He felt their sharp points digging into his skin.

Jesse licked the tight bud and fingered her, brushing her clit with every other stroke. He didn't want to finish her off too quickly, not when she could be writhing and squirming instead. Her nipple slipped from his mouth with a wet pop, and he spread her open with his fingers. She was perfect: wet and slick and dark pink. Just ripe and begging to be tasted.

He slid further down her body, resting his sore hand on her tit.

Harper spread her thighs further apart, opening herself to him, for his mouth. He kissed the warm insides of her thighs and she sighed dreamily. Her body arched when his mouth landed on her hot core.

Jesse took his time, licking her from top to bottom, savoring her wet arousal, just barely teasing her swollen clit with his tongue. He could feel her breathing turn to pants, feel the shaking of her plush thighs as they bracketed his face, like she was barely restraining herself from snapping them closed. He wished she would. He would suffocate in her cunt and die a happy man.

Jesse latched on to her clit and sucked; Harper whined, one of her hands grabbing his hair so hard it sent pain zipping down his spine, which only made his dick pulse. He sucked and licked until she was bucking her hips, fucking his face, and making that little whining keen that he loved so much.

She was so close, and Jesse knew just what she needed to finish. She needed to be filled. His cock ached with the urge to drive into her flesh, but he wouldn't do that to Harper. Not yet. She needed to come often, and loudly, before he gave her his cock.

Jesse used his fingers. She was dripping wet, so it was easy to plunge two inside her. Harper's hips moved faster, to match the pace of his sucking and the thrust of his fingers. He felt the flutter of her pussy that heralded the coming break of her release; her fingers tightened in his hair and she let out a long, strained "Fuccckkkk" as she orgasmed on his hand and his tongue.

Jesse pumped his fingers a few more times and licked her again for good measure, just so he could feel the aftershocks of her release.

Harper's hand dropped out of his hair as he pushed himself up to a sitting position, one leg braced on the floor. He needed to get his boots and pants off and sink into her flesh, but he stopped to admire the view.

She was still sprawled open in front of him, her eyes heavy lidded and sated, a pink flush over her cheeks and the tops of her breasts. She smiled up at him and Jesse thought it was the most beautiful thing he'd ever seen. He wanted to keep her like this forever, smiling up at him beatifically, her taste in his mouth. He wanted to bottle this feeling—a feeling of freedom, of lightness in his chest that he only felt around her.

He had revealed everything, told her his secrets, showed her the darkness, and she was still here, showing him her light.

Harper's tongue darted out to wet her lips, and she slid a hand down her belly. She let out a little laugh. "I think you gave me beard rash."

Jesse looked between her thighs. There were indeed red splotches spreading on her skin where his face had been.

He ran the tips of his fingers over the marks. Jesse's nostrils flared. A new, scary feeling bloomed in his chest. Possession. He wanted to mark her, brand her as his. He wanted to cover her with his cum, see it rope over her plump tits and stomach.

Jesse pulled at the hem of his flannel shirt and tugged it off and over his head. He was still basically fully clothed and he needed to be naked. He needed to feel her warm skin slide against his.

Harper's big brown eyes roved up his chest appreciatively and it made him want to preen. She sat up, her orange hair a riot of mussed curls. Her palms slid across his hips, thumbs brushing across the bunched muscles there, through the dark hair that trailed into the top of his unbuttoned jeans. His cock twitched behind the denim.

She slid his pants and boxers down his hips, finally freeing his straining cock.

Jesse groaned as her breath ghosted over the sensitive flesh, digging his fingers into the back of the couch, pain radiating up to his elbow. But it was overshadowed by her soft lips, her wet mouth.

He let her suck for several heartbeats before he stopped her with his fist in her hair. "No, baby girl, I need to fuck you."

Her dimples popped as she grinned at him.

Jesse moved to stand and Harper laughed. "Where are you going?"

He thought it would be rather obvious. He gestured towards the stairs. "To get a condom."

Harper chewed on her bottom lip, her legs and hips shifting to a more comfortable position on the couch, like she was suddenly nervous. The sunlight streaming in from the front windows sparked golden sunbursts in her eyes.

"What if we...didn't?"

Jesse's breath caught in his throat, even as his cock jumped and blood rushed so loudly through his head his ears felt muffled. Surely, he had misheard her.

"You want me to fuck you raw?" Jesse's voice was a harsh, disbelieving whisper.

He had never had sex without a condom, he'd never had a woman even ask. It wasn't safe, and he wouldn't do that to Harper. Even as the rational side of his brain listed excuses, the other, dark, primal side whispered that she was his. And, fuck him, he wanted to feel her raw, with no barriers. He wanted to feel the pulsing of her cunt as he unloaded his seed deep inside her.

"I have an IUD," she said softly, almost timidly, and Harper hadn't been timid a single moment since he'd met her. Her cheeks flushed an even deeper red. "I'm also...I mean I haven't...slept with anyone else. And I get tested regularly. I'm good...if...if you are."

Jesse stared at her as he pulled off his boots and pants, and she wiggled some more under his scrutiny.

"Is that what you want, Harper? You want me to fuck you raw? You want me to come inside you?"

Harper's limbs trembled and she let out a thin exhale. "Yes. God, yes." One of her hands creeped between her legs and her breath hitched as she played with herself.

Jesse was on her, pulling her hand away and holding it above her head. "That's for me. I'll give you the next orgasm, baby girl."

He cupped her chin with his other hand and brought their gazes level. Her eyes were round as moons. "You're fearless. Never be afraid to ask me for what you want." Jesse hesitated for just a heartbeat, because he feared the next thing out of his mouth would reveal too much of his soul, his heart. But he wanted her to know. "You can have anything you want from me."

The edges of her mouth pulled up in that mischievous little smile she had. "Then fuck me raw, Jesse Lee Abel."

The air punched out of his lungs as she pulled herself out of his loose grip and turned around on the couch, bracing one leg on the floor, presenting him with her plump ass and wet slit.

Jesse ran his hands across her shoulder blades, down her spine, over the delicious little dips down her sides, over the inked lines of the jewels and bows across her lower back. He squeezed the ample flesh of her ass, just to hear her breathing hitch. His cock was weeping, engorged and swollen. He ran the head through her folds and the skin-on-skin touch stuttered his heart in his chest.

Gripping his shaft, Jesse pressed inside, her sweet heat parting effortlessly, sucking him deep. Harper whined, and Jesse let out a string of rough curses as he seated himself fully inside her. There was nothing between them. Nothing but skin, but heat, but their ragged breaths, panting in tandem.

Jesse ceased to live, to draw air. There was nothing more important than Harper and her body and her pleasure.

He found purchase on her hips and started to move, going as slowly as he was physically capable of, dragging his cock across all her swollen, grasping flesh.

"God, I didn't think it could feel this good." Harper's voice was a soft, ragged drawl.

Jesse wanted to savor her, watch the space where their bodies connected, where he could see his cock disappear inside her, but Harper's hips were moving. She pulled off his cock and then pushed back again, her ass slapping against his pelvis, the movement rippling her skin.

Jesse let her set the pace, let her take her pleasure from him while he watched. He didn't deserve her. He knew that on a molecular level and the knowledge rankled. His sobriety felt like walking along the thin edge of a knife; one misstep would send him back into the abyss. And she deserved so much more than a man who was hanging on by a thread.

They were panting together, Harper's movements becoming sloppy and frantic. He squeezed her hips until she let out a gasping breath of air.

Jesse leaned forward, wrapping a handful of orange hair around his fist and tugging until her back bowed and her neck arched, until he could see her desperate eyes. Her tongue darted out to wet her lips; Jesse felt his own release building, a throbbing barrage that crawled up his spine. He wasn't going to last much longer like this, but he wanted her to come first. He wanted her to break apart on his cock.

He released her hair and slid that same hand down her back, Harper's skin pebbling under his touch.

"Make yourself come, baby girl. Make that sweet pussy squirt all over me."

Harper groaned. "Oh my God." Her hand shot down between her legs and Jesse knew when she found her clit because her pussy spasmed around him and he hissed at the pressure.

She rubbed herself in frantic strokes, tits swinging under her body. It was quite the sight, to watch her come undone while she was impaled on him.

Jesse matched his thrusts to the movement of her hand; they were fast and short, punching into her soft body.

Harper let out a strangled moan that was so loud he was sure her neighbors were in danger of hearing the sound. It was music to his ears. The pure, unadulterated sensation of her coming around his cock, the fluttering and spasming and clenching, was enough to make Jesse go cross-eyed with pleasure. Her cunt seemed determined to drag his own orgasm out, but he clamped down on the urge.

He fucked Harper through her orgasm until he physically couldn't stand it—it was only a couple more short thrusts—before he jerked out and spewed all over her ass and the small of her back. He groaned, short of breath, and pumped his dick with his hand until he felt drained of all life. Jesse's chest was covered in a thin layer of sweat.

Harper gave him a sassy look over her shoulder, one of her perfect brows raised. "Really?"

Jesse didn't even have the energy to reprimand her. He could barely breathe or think. All the blood that had rushed down to his cock had yet to return to his head. He was still gripping her hips. "Maybe next time."

He wasn't sure what had made him pull out at the last second but his cum was in ropes across her porcelain skin and it satisfied something deep inside him. He resisted the urge to spread it—barely.

Jesse cupped her cunt so abruptly Harper gasped and flinched; he ran his fingers over and through the messy folds. Not to arouse, but just because he wanted to feel her, feel the mess she'd made between her thighs.

"Why are you so fucking perfect?" he groused. Even to his ears, the words were spoken almost petulantly, like he was put out about that fact.

She laughed, the sound husky in her throat. "It just comes naturally to me." She grinned. "Care to get me a towel? I don't own this furniture and would rather not have to explain the...ejaculate...to the owners."

She looked at him over her round shoulder, face red-cheeked, hair a mess of disparate curls framing her face. She looked well-fucked and that made Jesse's heart contract even as his lips twitched.

He gave her ass a friendly swat as he got up from the couch and went to the kitchen to find a rag or a towel. He ran some warm water over the daisy yellow rag he'd found before ringing the excess water out and returning to the living room.

Harper was still in the prone position, her chin resting on her palm, patiently waiting for him to come back and clean up his mess. He ran the warm rag across her skin, trailing it with the tips of his fingers. Her skin shivered and pebbled and she made a little humming sound that would probably be the death of him.

"I love it when you touch me," she said, her voice soft and languid.

Finished with his task, Jesse tossed the used rag into their pile of clothes. Then he went back to the couch; Harper was in the middle of rising, but he wedged himself under her body, pulling her back down.

She squeaked with protest as he wrapped his arms around her shoulders and squeezed her hips between his thighs. He wedged one of the silly little decorative pillows under his head so he could gaze down at where she rested her chin on his abdomen.

"I'm going to squish you."

Jesse scoffed. "I can squat more than you, baby girl."

She nipped at his skin. "Okay, but that was like, years ago. You look a little out of shape to me."

Jesse couldn't help himself; he laughed, the sound unfamiliar and shaking his body, which shook Harper in turn. She was smiling up at him, part of her bottom lip stuck in her teeth.

She was still so young. She was still Teddy's only child. Teddy was still his boss. But Jesse wasn't sure he was going to be able to let her go. Not when she looked at him like she was happy, like she was home, like she was content.

Harper sighed, her hot breath ghosting over his bare skin. He could feel her heartbeat and it felt like hers was beating in time to his. She turned her head, snuggling her cheek into him.

"I want to stay," she whispered, so low he almost didn't catch it. Jesse's heart stuttered to a stop. He had been stroking her shoulder with his fingers, but those froze too.

Maybe she just meant she wanted to stay here, on this couch, in this moment.

"You…" Jesse had to clear his dry throat. He wasn't even sure what he wanted to ask. "You…that's what you want?"

"You told me never to be afraid to ask you for what I want. I want to stay here with you. Because of you."

Jesse swallowed again, watching as the movement bounced Harper's head. "What about…what about your job? Your friends? Your…life?" There had to be more important things to her than him. His chest was hurting. A headache had formed at his temples as he tried to riddle out her intentions.

She sat up abruptly, an elbow going into his ribs. "I can work from anywhere. Do you not want me to stay?"

Jesse was not good with words. He didn't know how to tell her he wanted that more than anything, more than air. He wasn't sure what words to use to express to her how much she meant to him, how quickly she'd burrowed herself in his skin.

The tips of his fingers traced her lips, the line of her chin and jaw, the column of her throat. He left his hand there, so he could feel the rapid thread of her pulse against his palm.

"You're mine, baby girl. You're not going anywhere."

Chapter Eleven

Harper

The gym was relatively quiet.

Harper was sitting with Raleigh on the couch in the lobby, helping her swipe through matches on a new dating app.

Raleigh had a quick and decisive swiping thumb. "No, no, no, not even if hell froze over."

"Oh, go back, he was cute."

"No, I went to high school with him.

"Ew."

"Right."

"Ohhh."

Raleigh paused on a profile of August, chewing on the inside of her cheek. His profile pic was one that Harper had taken, his smooth chest shiny with oil. He was smiling at the camera, even though the whole gym had tried to get him to stop smiling that day in an effort to break him out of his golden retriever energy.

"August, really?" Raleigh's ears went slightly pink and Harper grinned. "I mean, he is awfully cute."

Raleigh exited the app without making a decision on August's profile, Harper noticed.

"I don't make a habit of getting eaten out where I work."

Harper snorted. "I'm not sure that's how that saying goes."

"Trust me. It's better that way." Raleigh slipped her phone in the pocket of her leggings and got up to go back to the desk.

Harper thought about one of the things Jesse said last night. She hadn't been able to stop thinking about last night—everything they did, everything they said—but one thing in particular stood out to her.

He was worried about her leaving her friends. Harper *had* friends, but most of the friends she made in college went back to their hometowns or off to their after-college jobs, like she had.

Since she bounced around a lot, Harper was used to making fast but superficial relationships with people—colleagues, roommates, romantic partners—enough to go out for after-work drinks but nothing that she felt was deep. It was easy to leave, easy to move on to the next opportunity.

Cedar Creek felt different than it had at eighteen. It used to feel like a tomb, a place where ambition went to die. But something had changed these last couple months. Cedar Creek was homey, things could be built here—gyms, dreams, relationships.

She liked Raleigh, she liked the other regulars at the gym, she liked the cozy diner, and she liked the little bar. She liked her small rental.

Things felt different this time—she felt different about this place she used to call home but hated.

Jesse felt different too.

The way he looked at her, the way he touched her, the way he growled in her ear, and his perpetually grumpy scowl. They were small things, little things she didn't think she'd be able to give up. And she didn't want to. And if Jesse's declaration to her was any indication, he didn't want her to either.

"You're mine, baby girl. You're not going anywhere."

Raleigh coughed obnoxiously and Harper realized she just had been staring blankly at the wall for an unusually long time.

"You look like you have something to share," Raleigh said, with a suggestive arch of her brows.

Harper did want to share. Her chest felt stretched to bursting with the need to share what had happened and how she felt. Trusting Raleigh with this information would be a good first step on the road to friendship.

Harper sucked in a breath. "Okay, so you know about me and Jesse—"

"Who doesn't know about you and Jesse." She grinned and propped her elbows on the counter. "Are you finally gonna give me the saucy details?"

Harper's stomach sank. "You knew?"

"Wait. Was it a secret? Y'all were about as subtle as a brick to the face."

"Does everyone know?"

"Y'all probably shouldn't have spent so much time eye fucking each other and sneaking off if you didn't want people to know. And Ben is the biggest gossip in the whole town."

Something must have shown on Harper's face because Raleigh frowned, suddenly serious. "Did you not want people to know?"

Harper's chest felt tight, like she couldn't breathe. She didn't *not* want people to know, but they hadn't exactly been broadcasting their extracurriculars either.

"Are people...talking about us?" Harper didn't care if people gossiped, but she knew Jesse did. She knew he was hung up on her age. She knew he cared what her dad thought, even if she didn't. It would have been preferable for her to talk to Teddy first, but she could handle this. They could handle this, together.

"Just that y'all are cute together and you seem to be good for Jesse. I think he cracked a joke the other day. The boys were shocked, I tell ya."

Harper's cheeks heated at the compliment. She thought they were good together, too. She leaned a little closer, almost conspiratorially close, over the counter.

"I told him that I wanted to stay."

Raleigh's eyebrows shot up into her hairline. "What did he say to *that*?"

Harper felt her cheeks get even hotter, if that were possible. "He told me I was his."

Raleigh swatted her on the bicep and gasped. "No, he didn't. Stop. That's so romantic." She frowned, thoughtful. "You know, I didn't think he had that in him."

"He's a man of few words, but they tend to be the right ones."

"I'll say."

Harper lost her train of thought because her eyes suddenly caught on a commotion happening behind Raleigh's shoulder in the gym. There were people...running? And not on the designated running equipment.

Raleigh noticed Harper's gaze, whipping her head around, ponytail swinging aggressively. "What the fuck." She moved quickly to the glass doors, and Harper followed, hot on her heels.

There was indeed a commotion happening in the gym.

The crowd grew thick the closer they got to the ring. There were two men grappling on the floor, and unfortunately, Harper recognized them both.

Teddy was straddling Jesse's waist, attempting to get hits in on his face, but Jesse had his arms up in a defensive posture, not attempting to hit back, from what she could tell.

Her dad's aim was awfully erratic, but that was probably because he was in a fit, face red and apoplectic. He was also screaming.

"I should break your other arm, you fucking bastard. That's my daughter!"

Oh, God. Harper wanted to die. Just disappear. Melt right into the shiny concrete. Eyes shifted her way, now that she and Raleigh had joined the spectators.

Raleigh scoffed, her eyes rolling. "Men."

Harper had to agree. She glanced around. "Is no one going to stop them?"

She would be surprised if anyone heard her over her dad's expletives and vivid descriptions of things he wanted to do to Jesse and his offending penis.

Raleigh shrugged. "Probably not. Your dad's a legend."

"Right." And he was the boss, as Jesse was so fond of reminding her. No one probably wanted to risk turning his wrath on them.

Harper watched droplets of blood splatter the concrete.

"Okay, that's enough." She stepped towards the men, only to feel a hand on her arm.

"Harper." It was August, his panicked gaze flickering from her, to Raleigh, to the men on the floor.

Harper shrugged him off, marching purposefully towards her father. She grabbed a fistful of his shirt and tugged. "I said that's enough!"

She was ignored, Teddy's attempts to punch Jesse in the face jerking him away from her grasp. Jesse's gaze found her through Teddy's limbs and he frowned, his bottom lip split, a trail of blood down his chin.

And that pissed her off.

She grabbed her dad's shirt in both hands and heaved; she wasn't a small girl, surely Teddy could feel what was happening.

He didn't, or he was purposefully ignoring her tugging and yelling. "Dad, stop. Dad, fuck. Daddy, I love him!" she finally screeched.

And that was what finally caught his attention.

Teddy froze mid-punch and the sudden halt in movement threw Harper off-balance. She stumbled back a few steps before losing her balance and falling on her ass.

Harper's chest was heaving and the air was heavy, weighted, like the whole damn room was holding its breath waiting for whatever was about to happen next.

Teddy's angry glare slewed to her and he immediately deflated when he saw her sprawled on the ground.

"Harper—"

"Are you done now?" she snapped, getting up to her feet with an agility born of mortification. She brushed off the back of her leggings, crossed her arms, and glared.

The color drained from Teddy's face and he slowly got off Jesse like his limbs weighed tons. He offered a hand to help the other man up, but Jesse ignored it, getting to his own feet and brushing away blood with the back of his hand.

They both faced her with slumped shoulders like they were about to be scolded. She wasn't sure Jesse started anything, but she didn't mind giving him a piece of her mind anyway.

"You're grown fucking men," Harper spat. There was muffled laughter from behind her back, but then someone *oofed*, like they'd been elbowed in the ribs.

Her dad at least had the good sense to look ashamed of himself. He was flexing his hand, the one she assumed was used to sock Jesse in the jaw.

Jesse didn't seem to care that he'd just been pinned to the floor and still had blood on his chin. His heated eyes gazed at Harper with an intensity that made her want to squirm away while simultaneously making her belly heat. It was inappropriate for him to be looking at her like that in a room full of other people.

"Did you mean it?" Jesse rumbled, his voice a gravelly rasp.

Harper's heart was pounding furiously inside her chest; she could feel her rapid pulse in her neck, in her wrists.

"What?" she was practically gasping.

"Did you mean what you said? About loving me?" His growly voice was soft, but to her ears, it felt like it echoed through the tall ceilings of the gym.

Harper wasn't breathing, and neither was anyone else. Didn't he care that everyone was watching?

He apparently didn't, because suddenly he was moving towards her until their chests were barely a breath apart and Harper had to tip her head up to keep his gaze.

His thick fingers grasped her jaw, squeezing lightly. "Did you mean it?"

Harper licked her lips. There was no escaping this very public confession. She'd said the words on impulse, in an effort to get Teddy's attention, but even as they left her mouth, she knew the truth of them in her bones.

She hadn't planned on being the first to bare her soul, but she guessed it was good and too late now. She couldn't undo what she'd said.

"Yes. I did."

Jesse smiled, and it was like the sun breaking through clouds on a dark day. He leaned down and kissed her, his lips already slightly swollen. The kiss tasted sweet, with only a small tang of copper.

Harper found herself smiling against his lips because she knew this was where she belonged. His kiss and his smile and his fingers on her skin finally felt like home.

EPILOGUE

To his immense surprise, Jesse did not lose his job.

Teddy was rightfully pissed off, but softened as soon as he realized they were both serious and that Harper had decided to stay in town. She had taken Teddy out for a conciliatory lunch and allegedly explained the whole thing—although, Jesse hoped she did leave *some* details out. Teddy and Jesse's working relationship was back to normal after that, even if Teddy's eyes did track Jesse's every move anytime Harper was around.

Jesse got the distinct impression Teddy was just waiting for him to put one toe out of line before he started swinging again.

But Jesse wasn't worried.

Because he had no intentions of putting anything out of line any time soon. He was at her mercy. He had big plans for Harper. Plans that involved secluded vacation cabins and dense woods and no one around for miles and miles to hear her screams. And a ring. He had a plan for a ring, if she'd have him. And pumping her full of his seed, if that's what she wanted.

Harper groaned, her head falling back and Jesse reached up and pinched one of her pert, rosy nipples.

She was riding him, the sweet undulation of her hips a slow torture. A bead of sweat rolled down between her generous breasts; Jesse would lick that up later, after she'd found her first release on his cock.

Harper leaned back, bracing her palms on his thick thighs. Her chest heaved in short little pants and she was making that high-pitched keening moan that meant she was on the brink.

Jesse liked this position. He liked the way it stretched her body, strained her thighs. He liked that he could watch his flesh impale hers. He liked that she would take her pleasure this way.

Jesse let out his own groan as her cunt spasmed around him. Harper paused, her arms shaking, her pretty cunt grasping and fluttering through her orgasm.

With an extremely satisfied sigh, Harper dropped off Jesse's lap and sprawled beside him on the bed. A bed that smelled like her skin and her perfume.

"I'm still hard," Jesse said with a grin to the ceiling.

Harper snorted before sighing again. He felt her wriggling next to him, making herself more comfortable. "So?"

He looked at her. Her round cheeks were flushed and she grinned at him, daring him to do something about it. *Brat.*

"I'll discipline you for that later. But I have something for you now." Jesse rolled off the bed and found his jeans, pulling the key from his back pocket.

He held it up and Harper's forehead creased. "Looks like a key."

Jesse leaned over and dropped the key into her outstretched hand. "It's a key to my place."

The little lines on her forehead deepened and she rubbed her thumb over the shiny metal. She snorted when she noticed the Bluegrass Performance Center branded keychain. It was shaped like their logo, the outline of a flexing man's silhouette with a dumbbell underneath.

Her look of quiet consternation was not exactly the enthusiastic response Jesse was expecting. "Do you..." He cleared his suddenly dry throat. "Do you not want a key?" If her answer was no, then he had vastly misread the situation. An uncomfortable feeling snaked through his chest.

She was shaking her head, golden brown eyes welling with unshed tears. And he'd made her cry again.

Jesse knelt on the bed, grabbed her hand that still held his house key, wrapping his fingers around hers. "It's okay if you don't want it. If it's too soon. I just...I just didn't think you wanted to rent forever."

Harper choked on a short laugh. She snatched her hand from his and held the key to her chest, as if he'd take it away if she didn't protect it. His lips twitched.

"No, I accept. I will move in with you, Jesse Lee Abel."

Jesse's heart constricted even as his mouth curved in a broad grin. A phenomenon that seemed to happen a lot around Harper. "I love you," he said, just in case she hadn't figured that out yet.

Harper bit at her bottom lip, her eyes still slightly damp even as they flashed with mischief. "Fuck me like you love me, then."

Desire ran hot and heavy through his blood.

Jesse did not need to be told twice.

Afterword

Thank you for reading *False Finish*! I hope you enjoyed Harper and Jesse's story and are ready to prop up your feet and stay for a long time in Cedar Creek, Kentucky. A good time is guaranteed!

Reviews are one of the best ways to support an author, so I would love you forever if you left one (or even just some stars!) somewhere on the internet. Be sure you're following me for updates about the series. Who's next? You'll just have to wait and see!

Did you really, *really* enjoy this story and want to dive deeper into the Jessica-verse? I would be absolutely tickled if you joined me on Patreon! You can get free eBooks, sticker mailings, behind-the-scenes updates, bonus content, early access, art, and can start reading my unhinged paranormal romance serial, *Guilty As Sin*

About the Author

J.L. Minyard is the not-so-secret pen name of award-winning young adult author Jessica Minyard. Jessica is an author, poet, ISTJ, Sagittarius, and boy mom who lives and writes from the bluegrass.

Check out both her contemporary series:

Penn Warren University

Bluegrass Performance Center

For freebies, sneak peeks, and other updates, head to jessicaminyard.com to sign up for her newsletter or join her Facebook group or Patreon.

Follow her on social media:

facebook.com/jessicaminyardbooks

instagram.com/callmeshashka

tiktok.com/@jessicawritesromance

amazon.com/stores/J.L.-Minyard/author/B0B7R171CP

Minyard's Minions